AMERICAN ADVENTURES

Thomas

AMERICAN ADVENTURES

Thomas

BONNIE PRYOR

ILLUSTRATED BY
BERT DODSON

Morrow Junior Books

NEW YORK

Published by Morrow Junior Books
a division of William Morrow and Company, Inc.
1350 Avenue of the Americas, New York, NY 10019
www.williammorrow.com

Printed in the United States of America.

10 9 8 7 6 5 4 3 2 1

Library of Congress Cataloging-in-Publication Data
Pryor, Bonnie.
Thomas / Bonnie Pryor; illustrated by Bert Dodson.
p. cm.—(American Adventures)
Summary: In the early years of the Revolutionary War,
Thomas and his family escape a bloody massacre at Wyoming
Valley and endure innumerable hardships as they try to make their
way to Philadelphia.
ISBN 0-688-15669-X
1. Pennsylvania—History—Revolution, 1775–1783—Juvenile fiction.
2. United States—History—Revolution, 1775–1783—Juvenile fiction.
[1. Pennsylvania—History—Revolution, 1775–1783—Fiction.
2. United States—History—Revolution, 1775–1783—Fiction.
3. Frontier and pioneer life—Pennsylvania—Fiction.] I. Dodson,
Bert, ill. II. Title. III. Series: Pryor, Bonnie.
American Adventures.
PZ7.P94965Th 1998 [Fic]—dc21 98-9199 CIP AC

Contents

AMERICAN ADVENTURES

Thomas

ONE

---•---

A Warning

The beetle was big, black, and very ugly. Thomas Bowden took a stick and rolled it over on its back, then picked it up by one leg. The beetle wiggled frantically, and the large pincers snapped at the air. Carefully Thomas carried it to the barn and peeked around the corner. His sister, Emma, was sitting in the shade having a tea party with her doll. The tiny set of china dishes Aunt Rachel had sent all the way from Philadelphia was spread in front of her.

Emma's bonnet had fallen off and was lying in the dust, even though Mama insisted she wear it when she was outside. It was only the end of June, but the air was as hot and sticky as it was in late summer. Emma's brown curls were damp with sweat in spite of the shade from the barn. With his free hand Thomas ran his fingers through his own curly brown hair. People always remarked on how much he looked like Emma, even though she was only nine, a whole year younger—and a girl. They were not much alike in other ways, though. Thomas watched her pretending to sip a cup of tea. Mama hardly ever had to scold Emma, but he, on the other hand, was often into mischief. It wasn't that he meant to be bad. It was just that he was so curious about everything. Like the time he'd taken apart Mama's prized clock—he had just wanted to see how it worked. But then he had not been able to put it together again.

"I declare," Mama often teased. "I should have named you 'Why' Bowden instead of Thomas."

The beetle wiggled again, reminding Thomas of his plan. His bare feet made no sound as he crept up behind his sister. He dangled the beetle in front of her nose, grinning wickedly as she jumped up with an outraged squeal.

"Thomas!"

Thomas dropped the insect and tried to look innocent.

"He had a horrible creature, Mama," Emma whined. "He was going to put it down my dress."

"Was not," Thomas said. "I just thought you might be interested."

"He's lying," Emma said furiously. She brushed her unruly hair away from her face and made a fist at Thomas when she thought their mother wasn't watching.

Mrs. Bowden, however, had seen. "I wish you two would save your squabbling for a day when it isn't so warm," she scolded. "Don't I have enough to worry about?"

Thomas watched the beetle scurry away. "I'm sorry, Mama," he said. Thomas understood why she was worried. Twice in the last month travelers had stopped with disturbing news. Settlers in the north were being burned out of their homes, it was said, and even killed.

Thomas tried to push the reports from his mind. Four years before, the Bowdens had made their way to northeastern Pennsylvania and settled in the Wyoming Valley, named from a Delaware Indian word meaning "beautiful valley." The Indians weren't happy that so many white people were crowding onto their land. The settlers built forts up and down the Susquehanna River, a constant reminder that they were living on the frontier. Still, as more and more settlers poured into the valley and prospered, most people were too busy clearing land and planting crops to worry about Indian attacks.

Then came the war for independence against the British. It had been several months since Mr. Bowden left to join General Washington's army. News was slow getting to the valley, but Thomas knew that his father was fighting on the other side of the mountains, near Philadelphia. It didn't seem fair to have to worry about the war and Indian attacks, too. Especially when rumors said that it was other white Americans, still loyal to the British king, who were encouraging the attacks against their own countrymen.

Mrs. Bowden finished milking Ginny and gave her a pat. "Since you two have so much energy for arguing, you can do some more chores," she said as she stood up. "Emma, put your bonnet back on. Do you want to get freckled and brown? You can take Ginny to the barn. And bring Honey in from the pasture for the night. Thomas, you can carry the milk to the house."

Thomas opened his mouth to protest. After all, hadn't he been working for hours, chopping wood, carrying water, and tending the fire for his mother's monthly washing day—even hoeing the garden? His hands were blistered and his back sore. Then he looked at his mother's weary face and nodded.

Emma pouted. "Honey never wants to come to me," she complained.

"You just have to be firm with horses," Mrs. Bowden said. "Honey is lonesome since your father rode off on Black to join the army. That makes her cranky."

Emma put her arms around Ginny. "Good old thing," she crooned, patting her. "I like you much better than Honey."

Thomas could not resist another taunt. "Why don't you kiss her? You do look a lot alike."

Instead of answering back, Emma kissed the old cow's cheek with a loud smack. "You are just jealous because she doesn't like you."

"Eew," Thomas said. "Mama, she's kissing that old cow."

Mrs. Bowden placed a hand on her hip. Their usually gentle mother looked so stern that Thomas knew he had better not say any more. He picked up the heavy bucket and carried it carefully, trying not to let any of the milk slosh over the edge. "I wish Father would come home," he said, as he walked with his mother back to the house. Mr. Bowden had cut an extra door at the back of their cabin, making a shorter walk from the barn and garden. Thomas put down the milk bucket inside the door. Later his mother would skim off the good cream, which rose to the top, to be churned into butter. The milk would then be poured into a crock and taken to the springhouse to cool.

"I too, Thomas," answered his mother, as she picked his baby brother out of the cradle where he had been napping.

"The last time Father and I went to Fort Wyoming for supplies, I talked to Jacob Greene. He says his father thinks General Washington is a traitor. He says the rebels have no right to fight against the king."

Mrs. Bowden sat holding the baby in the small rocking chair by the huge kitchen fireplace. She leaned her head back and was quiet for so long Thomas thought she would not answer. At last she opened her eyes. "Jacob's father is a Tory. Some of

the patriots have been cruel to the Tories, tarring
and feathering them and driving them from their
homes because they've remained loyal to the king.
But there are still many good people who agree
with Mr. Greene. Your father, and most of the
other people in this valley, believe we are strong
enough to rule ourselves, instead of being ruled by
a king who lives far across an ocean."

"Still," Thomas said, "Jacob said the whole thing
started over a silly tax on tea. He said the king had
to get the tax money to help pay for sending soldiers to help fight the French. He said Samuel Ad-
ams got everyone angry about the tax but that it
was really a fair tax."

Mrs. Bowden nodded. "The tax was not unjust,"
she admitted. "But many felt that we should be the
ones to decide our taxes, not the king."

"Father should be here," Thomas repeated stubbornly. "In case the Tories come. Not off fighting
about some silly tax." For more than a year now
there had been rumors of an army gathering
strength in the north, just over the border in New
York. Its leader was a Tory named John Butler, and
people whispered that the powerful Iroquois na-

tion was uniting other tribes to join with him to drive the settlers from the frontier. Mr. Bowden had told Thomas that the Indians were willing to fight for the British because King George had promised to stop the colonists from settling new lands in the west.

Thomas's mother handed the baby to him while she stirred a kettle of good-smelling stew hanging on an iron hook over the fire. Thomas held his brother carefully. Little Ben was only three months old. He yawned and looked up at Thomas with bright blue eyes, then curled his tiny hand around Thomas's outstretched finger.

Mrs. Bowden lifted the kettle off the hook with a padded cloth and set it on the hearthstones to cool. "Your father would not have left us if he had believed we were in any real danger. We are a long way from the fighting."

She placed two wooden trenchers on the table. One was for herself and one was for Thomas and Emma to share.

Thomas put the baby back in his cradle. "Father's going to be surprised at how much Ben has grown," he said. Mr. Bowden had left to join General Washington right after the baby had been born. "I wish I could grow that fast."

Emma came into the house in time to hear him. "I'm almost as tall as you," she teased.

"Sometimes boys grow more slowly than girls," Mrs. Bowden said sympathetically. Just as she finished slicing bread to go with the stew, their old dog, Nobbin, got up from his place by the door and barked a warning. Thomas looked out the small front window. "Someone's coming."

Mrs. Bowden quickly reached for the gun hanging from a hook on the wall. Thomas's father often bragged that his wife could shoot straighter than he could. Mrs. Bowden peered out the window. Her husband had promised to put in a real glass window when the fighting was done. But for now it was covered with oiled paper, which did not let in much light. At night a shutter closed across the tiny opening.

Thomas's mother leaned the gun in the corner with a sigh of relief. "It's only Mr. Hailey," she said as she opened the door.

"How good to see you," she called. "My children and I are about to sit down for some venison stew."

She added proudly, "Thomas killed a deer last week."

Mr. Hailey was a farmer who lived about a mile up the river. He had stopped by often to check on them since Mr. Bowden had left. Usually he brought his daughter, Abigail, to visit with Emma.

Mr. Hailey dismounted but held the reins loosely as his horse grazed on some tall grass. He took off his hat and gave a courtly nod to Mrs. Bowden. "Thank you kindly," he said with a shake of his head. "That sounds good, but my wife probably has my own supper waiting." He reached into a leather saddlebag and handed a small package to Thomas. "It's that book I promised you," he said.

Thomas traced the letters printed in gold on the smooth leather spine. *"Gulliver's Travels,"* he read happily.

"It's by a man named Jonathan Swift," said Mr. Hailey. "I think you'll like it."

"Oh, thank you, Mr. Hailey. I'll take good care of it."

"I know you will." Mr. Hailey smiled. Then his face fell back into its usual dour expression. "That is only part of the reason I came," he said. "My wife is upset at these rumors we keep hearing. I reminded her that several months ago we spent a week at the Wintermoots' fort and nothing came of it. But she still insists that we leave. Tomorrow morning we're going to load what we can on my boat and head for the Forty Fort. Colonel Nathan Denison is in charge of the soldiers there. He is a good man. He'll know what to do if there is trouble."

Thomas always smiled at the fort's strange name. It had been built by the first forty settlers in the valley. Although there were several forts in the valley, it was the largest and most secure. Then he realized what Mr. Hailey was saying. If the Haileys left, there would be no one close enough to go to for help.

"Why do the Tories want to attack us?" he asked.

"The war is not going well for the British," Mr. Hailey answered. "If the Tories win on the frontier while General Washington is kept busy in the east, though, it may turn the tide in their favor."

"We have heard these rumors for a year," said Mrs. Bowden.

"This time I think my wife may be right," Mr. Hailey said with a grim shake of his head. "The Tories have been building boats all winter. It won't take them long to come down the river. People say that many Seneca warriors have joined them. The Tories may not be able to control the Indians once the fighting starts."

Mrs. Bowden was silent, but Thomas could guess her thoughts. He had been six years old when they crossed the mountains. Sometimes the trail was so rough that they lost precious time while his parents cleared away rocks and cut down trees so their wagon could get through. Finally they reached the Susquehanna. Father had built a raft, and they had nearly lost everything—including their lives— when it overturned in the fierce currents. But his parents hadn't given up, because they knew they could build a good life in the valley, and they had, through four years of backbreaking work.

Finally his mother spoke. "How would my husband feel if he returned and discovered that we had lost his home?"

"How much worse would he feel if he lost his family?" Mr. Hailey asked softly. He rubbed a bit of sweat from his forehead with the back of his hand.

Mrs. Bowden gave a stubborn shake of her head. "I'll think about it tonight. If we decide to go, I'll take the wagon. I'm not very fond of traveling on the water."

Mr. Hailey mounted his horse. "If you change your mind, be at the river at daybreak," he said. With a wave, he galloped off in the direction of his own cabin.

Mrs. Bowden stared after Mr. Hailey until he disappeared from sight.

Thomas stood beside her. "Don't worry, Mama. If anyone comes, I can fight. I'm almost as good a shot as Father."

"Shooting a deer and shooting a man are two different things," Mrs. Bowden said sharply. "And it won't come to that. Now let's go back and finish our supper."

TWO

———— • ————

Shadows in the Night

Thomas loved summer evenings. On winter nights he and Emma usually went to bed right after supper. It was too dark to do much else. The candles Mrs. Bowden made from tallow were smoky and smelled bad. The beeswax candles she bought from the traders who came up the river were too expensive to use for everyday. In summer, however, the longer days gave him and Emma some free time in the evening after the chores were all done.

What they loved best was wading in the stream that flowed under the springhouse, keeping foods from spoiling, even in the hottest weather. Sometimes they followed the stream as it wound its way through the fields, eventually emptying into the Susquehanna. The river was wide and the current too swift in places for swimming, but the stream was perfect for a cooling splash.

Tonight, however, Mrs. Bowden insisted that they stay near the house. Emma pestered Thomas into playing a halfhearted game of tag. It was hard with Nobbin around. Every time one of them hid, Nobbin went straight to the spot and stood there, wagging his tail until the hidden person was found. Finally, tired of the game, they sat under a tree near the cabin door. Thomas stretched back and looked at the sky.

"Do you ever wonder why the sky is blue?" he asked.

Emma looked up. "It just is," she said, shrugging her shoulders.

"And the sun," Thomas mused. "Today is so hot you can hardly stand it. But that same sun is there in winter and the air is cold. Why is that, do you suppose?"

Emma shook her head. "I've wondered about that, too," she admitted.

Thomas rolled over on his stomach and watched

an ant scurry away with a tiny crumb. "Why do ants live together when the other bugs don't?"

"Why are you so curious?" Mrs. Bowden said, smiling, as she stepped out to call them in.

"Someday I'm going to know all those things," Thomas bragged as he followed his mother inside.

"Good," said Mrs. Bowden, giving him a little hug. "Then you can come back and teach me."

Later their mother read aloud from the family Bible. It was the only book the Bowdens owned, and Thomas had heard the stories many times.

"You read for a while," Mrs. Bowden said, handing the book to Thomas.

"I wish we had a lot of books, like Mr. Hailey," Thomas remarked as he turned the well-worn pages. Thomas's mother had taught him to read, although he still stumbled over some of the biblical names.

Mrs. Bowden smiled. "I asked your father to bring back some books for you," she said.

Thomas could hardly contain his happiness. "What kind of books will he bring? How many? Do you think he will buy *Robinson Crusoe*?" This was one of the books on Mr. Hailey's bookshelf.

Mrs. Bowden held up her hand. "You will have to wait and see," she said with a chuckle. "Right now it is nearly dark and you two need to go to bed."

Reluctantly Thomas and Emma obeyed. "If there is a war, will we still get a school?" Emma asked as they walked up the narrow staircase to their attic sleeping loft.

There had been talk of building a schoolhouse in the tiny settlement called Kingston, near the Forty Fort. It was a long way from the Bowden farm, but Thomas's father had agreed to let them ride Honey when she wasn't needed for plowing.

Thomas shrugged. "Maybe not," he said glumly. "A teacher won't want to come where there is fighting."

Emma sighed, but Thomas knew she was not unhappy for the same reason he was. Emma was looking forward to school so that she could see her friend Abigail every day.

In spite of the sticky summer heat, Thomas fell asleep almost as soon as he stretched out on his bed. Downstairs, Ben still slept in a cradle close to their mother.

The baby was fussy. Thomas heard his mother's comforting voice singing softly as he drifted off. He awoke sometime later and sat up, wondering what had awakened him. The little house was silent. Emma tossed restlessly. He wondered if she was having bad dreams. Perhaps she had made some sound in her sleep, and that was what he had heard.

His body was damp with sweat. In winter the soft feather quilt that his mother had made to cover the straw mattress felt warm and cozy. But tonight it just made him feel hotter.

Thomas got up quietly and opened the shutters covering the tiny window in the attic loft. He felt uneasy without quite knowing why. Perhaps it was only Mr. Hailey's warning, still fresh in his mind. He looked out over the Bowden farm. When they had first come, neighbors had helped raise the house and barn. Then began the work of clearing the land. Acre by acre, Father had cut down trees, using some of the wood for furniture and fences and burning the rest. That first spring they planted corn around the tree stumps. With fall—and into the winter, too, when the ground wasn't frozen—

came the brutally hard work of digging around the stumps and then, with Black and Honey, wrenching them from the earth. So far Mr. Bowden had managed to clear nearly fifty acres.

Mama is right, Thomas thought. It would be terrible to give up the land now.

The moon was nearly full, and in its light everything looked calm and peaceful. Thomas started to turn away. Then he froze. There was a movement in the orchard next to the barn. It was the briefest shadow, a blurred shape, too quick to tell what it was. Thomas stared at the spot, but it did not appear again. An owl hooted from the forest. Then there was an answering call from the shadowy thicket.

Mr. Bowden had taught Thomas how to imitate some of the birds and animals. There was something not quite right about the owl's call. He held his breath, listening, but the sound did not come again.

Thomas reached up, closed the shutters, and latched them in place. He slipped on his pants and had a foot on the ladder when he became aware that Emma was awake.

She leaned up on one elbow. "What is it?" she whispered. "Is something wrong?"

"Go back to sleep," Thomas told her. "I'm just going to get a drink of water."

Thomas climbed down, trying to decide what to do. Should he wake his mother and tell her about the owl with a shadow that seemed the size of a man?

"Did they wake you, too?" asked his mother's quiet voice. She was sitting in the rocker. His father's gun lay across her lap, pointed at the door.

Nobbin was sitting beside his mother's chair. A low growl rumbled in his throat, but Mrs. Bowden's hand restrained him from barking.

Thomas sat on a small stool at her feet. "If only we had another gun."

"If we are attacked, I doubt if two would hold them off any more than one," Mrs. Bowden said gently. She pointed to a crack in the shutter. A faint pink glow in the sky told of the approaching dawn. "I think we have made it through this night without harm. I've been thinking about Mr. Hailey's words. As soon as we've eaten, we'll leave. Go and wake your sister."

Thomas scrambled up the ladder and yelled at Emma. "Get up. Mama says we're going."

Emma jumped up. Although her eyes were still puffed with sleep, she quickly pulled her summer dress over her sleeping shift and smoothed her hair. Thomas went back down the ladder and looked around.

"What shall we take?" he asked.

Mrs. Bowden hesitated. "It's miles to the fort. We'll only take a little food and our valuables." She glanced around the tiny cabin, taking inventory. "My silver candlesticks, the Bible."

"What about Ginny?" Emma burst out as she came down the ladder. "And the hens?"

"We can tie Ginny to the back of the wagon," Thomas offered.

Mrs. Bowden nodded. "The chickens will be able to scratch up enough food for a while. They will stay near. Maybe we won't be away that long," she added brightly.

Thomas was glad that they would be taking Ginny. The old cow had been with them for as long as he could remember, and though he often grumbled at the early morning milking and teased his sister for hugging her, he was fond of her, too. He loved the way steam rose from her breath on frosty mornings and how she patiently watched him with soft brown eyes as he spread a pile of hay for her to eat while he milked.

"Hitch up Honey," Mrs. Bowden said. "By the time you are done, we will be ready to go."

Nobbin padded softly to his side, and Thomas gave him a grateful pat. He didn't want to admit how nervous he was about going outside by himself. Thomas wasn't sure how much protection the old dog would be, but he felt better just to have Nobbin with him.

"Wait," called his mother. Thomas stopped, his hand on the door. His mother picked up the gun and pulled the latch.

Mrs. Bowden stepped outside and swung the gun around while she searched for any danger. Thomas felt an ache deep inside as he looked out over the Bowden farm. Beside the barn was his mother's vegetable garden with its neat rows of squash, beans, and corn nearly ready to harvest. The small orchard was at one end. Mrs. Bowden had carefully wrapped the tiny trees, a gift from her sister in Philadelphia, and brought them when they came to the valley four years before. This spring, for the first time, several of the trees had been covered with fragrant white blossoms, and now they were dotted with tiny green apples and plums.

Beyond the orchard grew fields of grain stretching to the banks of the river. In the other direction a faint early-morning mist nearly hid the rugged mountains.

Mrs. Bowden handed Thomas the gun. "Take this with you. Go quickly," she said.

Thomas gripped the gun tightly as he ran toward the barn. Three deer were standing in the garden, nibbling on his mother's tender vegetable plants. When they saw Thomas, they were off in a flash, white tails held high in alarm. With a gleeful squeal, Nobbin set off in pursuit.

"Nobbin! Come back," Thomas shouted, knowing it was useless. Even though he could never catch the fleet-footed deer, Nobbin would chase them until he was exhausted before he'd give up. Sometimes he was gone for hours, and when he returned, he'd be covered with burrs and looking sheepish. Already he was out of sight, hidden in the tall grain.

Even though it was just barely daybreak, the air was already warm. He tried to tell himself that the sweat that trickled down his forehead was from the sun. He slowed to a walk, wiping his palms on his pants.

When nothing had happened by the time he had reached the gate to a small corral at one side of the barn, Thomas's heart stopped pounding and he let out a long breath. If it had been Indians he'd seen during the night, they must have been just passing through. Maybe they were headed for the river. Thomas often saw them paddling downstream in their silent canoes.

Although the gate was closed, the rawhide loop that secured it to the fence post was not in place. "Emma," he muttered under his breath, remembering that Emma had taken Ginny to the barn. Thomas slipped through the gate. The wooden bar that locked the barn door was lying uselessly on the ground, and the door was slightly ajar. Even Emma would not have been that careless. What if the shadows had been there to steal Honey? He threw open the barn door.

Honey was not in her stall. While he had stayed in the safety of his house, shaking at shadows, someone had stolen his father's horse. Thomas hit one fist in his other hand. Without Honey, they would have to walk all the way to the fort. It was already past dawn, too late to go with the Haileys.

And what about Ginny? He thought of her just as he became aware of an unpleasant odor, something that reminded him of... what? He sniffed the air. Then suddenly he knew, and his stomach did a funny lurch. Blood! It was the coppery smell of fresh blood.

THREE

Captured

Slowly, reluctantly, Thomas crept around the corner of the stall, dreading what he knew he would see.

Ginny was lying near some stacks of hay. At first it looked as though she was merely sleeping, but as Thomas drew near he could see that her throat had been cut and her soft brown eyes were glazed over. A dark circle of blood had dried into the earthen floor. "Oh, Ginny," he moaned. It wasn't bad enough to steal Honey. This unspeakably cruel thing had been done to taunt them, to let them know how close they had been to death themselves.

A skep made of coiled straw sat not far from the

barn. This was where his mother kept bees. Thomas heard the soft buzzing, the only sound that broke the silence. A prickly feeling crawled along his skin. He strained to see into the dark corners of the barn. The first cutting of hay was stacked neatly where he had found Ginny. Mr. Hailey had helped them bale some hay for the animals' winter feed. It had been hot, itchy work, and Thomas remembered sadly how he'd wished that day that they didn't have a cow. "I didn't mean it, Ginny," he whispered, glancing back at her lifeless body.

Thomas felt the door behind him. He crouched down, searching for any sign of movement in the woods. Did unseen eyes watch him even now? For a moment Thomas remained paralyzed, afraid to cross the distance to the house. Then slowly an icy anger replaced the fear. He stood up boldly in the open doorway, holding his gun. "Cowards!" he shouted. "What kind of man makes war on cows?"

A blue jay screeched from his perch on the fence. Thomas swung the gun around and nearly fired before he realized what it was. The bird continued to scold as it flew away, not knowing how close it had come to death. Feeling foolish, Thomas lowered the gun. Then, taking a deep breath, he sprinted back toward the house. He had already reached for the door when he heard a man speak. For an instant he thought it was Mr. Hailey, waiting for them after all. Then he heard his mother's pleading voice.

Crouching, he eased the door open just a crack. His mother, holding the baby, was facing him; yet she gave no sign. The man's back was turned, his musket resting carelessly across one arm. Emma was also there. She stepped closer to her mother, but except for a slight widening of her eyes, she gave no clue that she saw Thomas. Thomas did not have to see the bright green coat the man was wearing to know that he was part of John Butler's army.

Thomas raised his gun slowly. Would he have the strength to shoot? Even while he took aim, he wasn't sure. He wished the man was not standing so close to his mother. What if he missed?

Something hard pressed against his head. "Well, now," said a rough voice in his ear. "What do we have here?"

Thomas felt himself jerked to his feet by the

back of his shirt. The gun flew out of his hands and clattered to the ground.

The greencoat inside the cabin whirled around. He raised his musket and then, when he saw Thomas, slowly let it down.

"I found this pup outside," the second man said, shoving Thomas roughly into the cabin. He waved his pistol at Thomas. "This boy was getting ready to take a shot at you."

The soldier who had captured Thomas was an older man with hard eyes. He snatched up Thomas's gun and motioned him to stand near his mother. Thomas obeyed, thinking bitterly of the lost chance for escape.

"Outside," the soldier with the musket ordered. They had no choice but to obey. Mrs. Bowden grabbed several pieces of dried venison she'd been wrapping for the journey. The soldier scowled but allowed her to slip them into her apron pocket. She carried Ben silently through the front door of the cabin, and Emma and Thomas followed behind.

The soldier who had been talking with their mother was younger, just barely grown. He stood with his feet braced apart as though to steady himself. Thomas noticed that his hand shook a little, and he avoided their eyes as though he were ashamed.

Several other mounted men waited on the trail. Thomas silently scolded himself for being so careless. They must have arrived while he was in the barn with Ginny.

As though she knew what he was thinking, Emma leaned close. "There are too many of them. They would have just killed you."

Thomas sighed. She was right, of course. There were too many.

Two of the horsemen also wore Tory green, but the third man was an Indian. Thomas looked at him, curious in spite of his fear. From his nose down, the man's face was painted black. His head was shaved on both sides, but a thatch of hair had been left in the middle. It was pulled back and braided at the back of his head. He was wearing a green Tory jacket, but it did not seem to match his fierce appearance. He stared indifferently as the older soldier lit a torch and, without a word, threw it on the cabin roof. A thin curl of smoke drifted up; then there was a tiny *poof* as the dry thatch caught flame. They were forced to watch as the fire crackled into a raging blaze. Thomas heard a soft moan escape from his mother's tightly pressed lips. A second torch quickly turned the barn into a raging inferno.

"Ginny," Emma cried. Thomas caught her hand. "It's all right," he lied. "I set Ginny and Honey free."

The young soldier looked startled. He looked at Thomas; then, with a guilty look, his gaze drifted away. Thomas glared at him. He knew about Ginny, Thomas was sure. Perhaps he was even the one who had done it.

Emma hid her face in her mother's skirt. Mrs. Bowden patted her distractedly as she shifted Ben in her arms. "How shall I care for my children then?" she asked. Tears brimmed in her eyes.

"You rebels should have thought of that before you started this war," the older soldier said gruffly.

"This is how the king makes war? By starving children?" His mother's voice was scornful in spite of her tears.

The thought of Ginny made Thomas bold. His voice shaking with anger, he said, "If my father was here, he'd—"

Thomas did not finish his threat. His mother's

hand clamped down on his shoulder, warning him to stay quiet. At the same time the older soldier raised his pistol, pointing it directly at Thomas.

The older man's coat was dusty and worn, as though he had been a soldier for a long time. To Thomas he said, "You rebels started this war. Don't look for pity from me. I lost a brother at Breed's Hill. Be glad you are only losing your house."

Satisfied that the fire had spread too far to control, he swung himself up on his horse and, motioning for the younger soldier to follow, trotted to the road, where the others waited silently. "Carry this warning, woman," he called back as they galloped away. "We are reclaiming this valley for the king and his subjects."

The barn roof collapsed in a shower of sparks, catching the field of wheat behind it. Mrs. Bowden appeared dazed. Handing Ben to Emma, she grabbed the baby's blanket and began beating uselessly at the spreading flames. Thomas clutched at her arm.

"Mama. Stop. It's no use," he shouted over the roar of flames. "We have to get to the river."

"Look," shouted Emma. From the direction of

the Hailey farm a thin trickle of smoke drifted lazily to the sky.

Smoke was making their eyes water and their throats burn. Still holding on to the charred blanket, Mrs. Bowden seemed to regain her senses. Taking Ben from Emma, she motioned to the river. "Run," she shouted.

Tiny tongues of flame chased them as they bolted for the cool waters of the Susquehanna. They gasped for breath in the smoky air. Ben was screaming. Mrs. Bowden buried his tiny face against her shoulder, shielding him from the hot sparks carried in the heavy smoke. Emma stumbled and fell. Thomas pulled on her arm, helping her up.

At last they reached the riverbank and slid down into the muddy water. Mrs. Bowden dipped the baby into the water, protecting him from the flames while he screamed in protest.

There was a small island in the middle of the river. It wasn't far, but Thomas knew that the water was too deep for them to make it all the way across. If the fire jumped the river, they would be trapped. But luck was with them. The fire died as quickly as it began, burning itself out along the muddy banks.

Shivering in spite of the warm day, Thomas waded out of the water and climbed the riverbank. Silently his mother and Emma followed. Across the acres of burned and ruined crops, he could see the stone chimney, all that was left of their home.

"It was just a house," Mrs. Bowden said with a grim look back. "A house can be rebuilt." With a determined shake of her head, she turned her back and headed for the safety of the fort.

FOUR

A Dangerous Trail

For the first mile or two they walked in glum silence, taking turns carrying Ben. At last, near a bend in the river, they came upon a grassy meadow. Mrs. Bowden sat down wearily on a stone and nursed the baby, rocking him in her arms until he slept.

Thomas glanced at the sun while he waited, trying to think. It was almost directly overhead, making it nearly noon, and they were still many miles from the fort. The soldiers had burned their house but had not harmed them. Any Indians they met along the trail might not be so generous.

"Maybe we should go to the Wintermoot fort," he said. "It's closer."

His mother shook her head. "The Wintermoot

family has Tory sympathies. Your father warned me not to trust them. It is little more than a cabin with a wooden wall around it, not much protection anyway. We will go to the big fort. There will be soldiers there and food. It's farther, but we'll be much safer."

"Where's Nobbin?" Emma suddenly wailed.

Thomas tried to remember when he'd last seen the old black dog. Had he been in the house when the soldier tossed the torch? Then suddenly he remembered.

"He ran off chasing a deer," he told his sister. "He'll be all right." He tried to sound more confident than he felt.

"We need to get away from the river," Mrs. Bowden said. "We'll be too easy to spot walking out in the open."

"There's a trail," Emma said.

Thomas shook his head. "Not the trail. What if we ran into more Tory soldiers?"

Mrs. Bowden nodded. "We'll have to make our way through the woods. At least we'd have a chance to hide. It will slow us down, but it will be safer."

"I'm awfully hungry," Emma said softly.

Mrs. Bowden reached into her apron pocket and pulled out the small hunks of dried venison. "There will be food at the fort," she said, dividing it three ways.

Thomas tore off a bite and chewed slowly, enjoying the salty taste as he led the way. The woods were thick. Vines twisted between trees, and bramble bushes scratched at their legs. Thomas tried to clear a path for his mother and sister, but it was nearly impossible without an axe. It was hot. Sweat trickled down his back. Blackflies and gnats circled, biting unmercifully at the back of his neck and at his face.

Thomas looked back at Emma. Normally she would have been whining and crying at such discomfort. But today he was amazed at her strength. She marched along bravely, without a word of complaint.

Thomas tried to think of a way to cheer her. "What gets bigger when you cut from both ends?" he asked.

"That's silly," Emma retorted. "Nothing gets bigger if you cut it from both ends."

"Except a ditch," Thomas said with a sly grin.

"Oh, you," Emma sputtered. But she smiled a little as they walked along.

Thomas carved a passage about midway between the river and the path. Through the trees they occasionally caught a glimpse of the river, often enough to be sure they were still heading in the right direction. Thomas worried about the noise they made as they pushed their way through the brush.

Suddenly they heard a joyful barking. A black streak wiggled from the underbrush and jumped at them.

"Nobbin," Emma cried, kneeling to hug him. "Mama, look. Nobbin found us."

Mrs. Bowden patted Nobbin's head, but Thomas noticed her worried frown and understood. If Nobbin were to bark at someone along the path, they could be discovered. "He'll be quiet," Thomas assured her. "I'll watch him."

His mother nodded. Nobbin ran a few paces ahead, stopping to smell every tree and rock in the forest. They walked on, trying to stay as silent as possible.

The forest suddenly thinned and they crossed a flat bluff close to the river.

"Get down," Mrs. Bowden suddenly hissed. She pushed them down behind the brush. Emma started to protest, but Mrs. Bowden held one finger to her lips. "Indians," she mouthed.

Nobbin's ears perked up, and a rumble started deep in his throat. Thomas grabbed him just in time and peeked out from their meager cover.

There were two of them, their faces painted black like that of the Indian with the Tory soldiers. They were paddling a canoe silently up the river. Nobbin struggled in his arms, but Thomas held him tightly. He kept one hand over the dog's muzzle so he couldn't bark.

It was Ben and not Nobbin who nearly gave them away. As they crouched behind the bushes, the baby gave a thin, wavery cry, not yet the full-blown bellow that sometimes came when he was made to wait for his feeding. Awkwardly, still in her crouching position, Mrs. Bowden rocked him and he quieted.

Thomas sat up and peered around the bushes. The warriors had paused, paddles still in the water. One of them pointed to the shore and said something in a harsh whisper.

Thomas watched as they maneuvered their canoe toward shore. He saw the panic in his mother's eyes. They were trapped. If they stayed in the brush, they surely would be found. And even with a head start they would never be able to outrun the fleet Indian warriors, not with Ben.

Motioning for Emma to hold Nobbin, Thomas cupped his hand over his mouth and growled. He ended the growl with a high-pitched screech, hoping he sounded like a wildcat. Thomas had heard a wildcat the last time he went hunting with his father. He'd been practicing the sound, hoping to scare Emma with it someday. Rabbits sometimes made a sound like a baby's cry when they were hurt. With luck the warriors would think a wildcat had caught one for his supper.

The canoe slowed a few feet from shore. The first warrior spoke again and laughed. The second man hesitated. Then he too laughed. Their paddles sliced through the water, and a minute later they had slipped around a bend and out of sight.

"That was so clever," Emma said, nearly bouncing with relief.

His mother's smile was strained. "We've still got a long way to go," she said.

Thomas peered at the sun, sinking low on the

horizon. His stomach growled. The only food he had had all day was the small piece of dried meat. Trying not to think of his empty stomach, he turned and plodded along determinedly.

It was after suppertime when they reached the fort. They smelled it first, a friendly smell of horses and wood smoke.

"What if they think we're Indians?" Emma asked, grabbing his arm as they emerged from the trees.

Thomas stopped in his tracks. Emma was right. They were sure to have guards. Mrs. Bowden handed Thomas the baby. She cupped her hands and loudly shouted, "Hello, is anybody there?"

A gruff voice shouted back. "Who goes there?"

"It's Ellen Bowden and her children," Mrs. Bowden shouted. "We've been burned out."

"Are you on the side of King George or freedom?" came an answering call.

"I am a patriot," Mrs. Bowden said proudly. "My husband is fighting with General Washington."

At that, the gates swung open, and helping hands rushed out to lead them in.

FIVE

The Forty Fort

The fort was surrounded by a double row of thick wooden poles rising nearly twelve feet. Overhead, soldiers patrolled along a walkway. A square-shaped blockhouse jutted out over the walls. The soldiers' barracks were in each of the four corners of the fort and along the wall closest to the river.

At the back of the fort were the animal barns, where the officers' horses were stabled. A few cattle were penned nearby. Several cabins clustered directly across from the soldiers' barracks. Their chimneys faced the inner courtyard, to protect the fort's outer walls from the danger of fire.

Emma coughed and tried to cover her nose with her sleeve. "It's so dusty," she complained.

The little family wound their way through a forest of tents crowded into the open area in the middle of the fort. It was difficult to make sense of the confusion. People milled about, talking in anxious groups. Families gathered around campfires, their household belongings stacked like firewood beside them. Thomas saw an old lady, dressed in her Sunday best, serenely sitting in a rocking chair outside her tent, while several small children whooped and hollered around her.

Thomas recognized some of the men gathered around the barracks. They were the local militia, made up of men from the valley. Only a few of the officers wore uniforms—and those were of homespun cloth—but most of the soldiers were heavily armed.

Here and there a soldier on leave from the Continental Army stood out in his snappy blue coat. Thomas wished his father was among them. The men worked while they talked, cleaning their guns or mending torn uniforms. Thomas noticed a boy with curly red hair watching a group of soldiers playing cards.

A plump, motherly woman hurried over to them.

"Are you the new people?" she asked. "I heard someone just arrived."

Mrs. Bowden nodded. "Our home was burned. We walked all day to get here."

"You must be exhausted," the woman exclaimed. "We're low on food, but I think we can find you something."

The woman took Ben from Mrs. Bowden's arms. "Well now, isn't this a sweet little one," she crooned. "I'm Mary Muldoon. My family has been here about a week. They've cleared out two of the barracks for us settlers. We'll find you a spot and get you some supper. I've got some salve that might help with those bites, too."

After a few feeble protests, Mrs. Bowden stumbled wearily after her, motioning the older children to follow. Thomas suspected that his mother was grateful to have someone else take charge. Mrs. Muldoon was nearly as round as she was tall. Tiny laugh lines crinkled the leathery skin around her eyes and mouth. "The Indians use bear grease to keep away the gollynippers," she said as she rummaged through a trunk. "Smells bad, but it works." In no time at all their faces were covered with a comforting salve, and they had been given a place to sleep. Mrs. Muldoon fetched several bowls of hot stew. She chattered cheerfully all the while. Even Nobbin had been given a bone. He sprawled outside the barracks, chewing happily.

"I don't know how I can repay you," Mrs. Bowden said.

"Nonsense," Mrs. Muldoon scolded. "Someone helped me when I first arrived. You can help the next person. You'll be safe enough here," she added. "We've got over three hundred fighting men and more coming each day."

Thomas looked around while he ate. Now that the fearful walk was over, he felt only excitement. The fort was fairly bursting with people. Living on the farm, he and Emma seldom had a chance to meet other people. He saw Emma eyeing some girls her age playing a game, hopping on one foot in some squares marked off in the dirt. Other children were running through the groups of worried-looking adults, playing tag.

"Do you think I will be able to meet some of the girls?" Emma asked.

"As soon as we've rested a bit," Mrs. Bowden answered, just as an officer approached them.

"Colonel Denison would like to ask you a few questions, Mrs. Bowden. If you are not too tired."

Mrs. Bowden stood up wearily. "I'll be happy to talk to him." She handed the baby to Emma and motioned for Thomas to go with her.

The soldier led them to a small room in the officers' quarters. A long, rough table was in the middle, nearly filling the crowded room. Officers of the militia sat on benches or crude wooden chairs. Others stood or leaned against the walls. A tall man entered the room. By his bearing, Thomas guessed that this was Colonel Denison. He introduced himself to Mrs. Bowden and offered her a chair, sat down beside her, and leaned forward, eager to hear her story.

Thomas stood close to his mother. He glanced around while she recounted the day's events. Some of the men looked angry, and Thomas had the feeling they'd been arguing before he and his mother entered the room.

Colonel Denison listened calmly, while some of his officers paced nervously back and forth. Finally,

Mrs. Bowden said, "I wish we could be of more help, but we saw only a few soldiers."

A bearded man jumped up and pounded on the table with his fist. With a start, Thomas realized it was Lazarus Stewart, the famous Indian fighter. Mr. Bowden had pointed him out at Fort Wyoming.

"This is just what I said. We're sitting safely in this fort while a handful of Tories and Indians are burning our homes," the man shouted fiercely.

"We don't know how many there are," Colonel Denison answered calmly. "From the reports I've had, the whole army might be here."

"Then where are they?" Lazarus Stewart growled.

"Let's allow Mrs. Bowden and her son to go before we discuss this further." Colonel Denison's eyes flashed with anger, but his voice was kind when he spoke to Thomas and his mother. "You are lucky to have survived," he said. "We are getting reports that others have not been so fortunate. Your information will help us reach a decision. The green uniforms tell us that Tories have indeed arrived." He walked them to the door and thanked them. "Don't worry," he said. "You'll be safe here."

"May I look around for a while?" Thomas asked his mother as they stepped outside.

"I would think even you'd be tired tonight," Mrs. Bowden said with a smile.

"I am," Thomas admitted. "I won't be very long."

"Just a quick look, then," his mother agreed as she left him.

Thomas walked around the fort, enjoying the noise and excitement. He had never seen so many people gathered in one place. The red-haired boy Thomas had noticed earlier was leaning against the rough log wall of a barracks. A distance away some soldiers were oiling their guns. One of them called, "Hey, Eben, come and sit with us."

The soldier had the same red, curly hair as the boy, and Thomas guessed he might be an older brother.

Swaggering a little, Eben hurried over, bumping into Thomas and nearly knocking him to the ground. "Watch where you're going, Shorty," the boy smirked.

Thomas scrambled up, his hands tightening into fists. "You bumped into me," Thomas said. "And my name is *not* Shorty."

The boy laughed. He was at least a head taller than Thomas. He looked at Thomas's fists. "Oh, a fighter are you, Shorty?"

"If I have to be," Thomas said. "And stop calling me Shorty. My name is Thomas."

The boy grinned. "Tell you what, short Thomas. Apologize and we will forget the whole thing."

SIX

─·•·─

A New Friend

Thomas sputtered. "I'll not apologize. You knocked into me." He swung his fist at Eben, but the bigger boy was faster. He shot out an arm and pushed Thomas's head, keeping him at such a distance that his fist flayed empty air.

"You should not have been in my way," Eben said, still holding him back.

Thomas swung once more, but again he struck only air. The boy grinned at him. "I'll wager we look pretty foolish," he said. "I'll tell you what. You apologize for being in my way, and I'll apologize for knocking into you."

Thomas let his fists relax. Eben's smile was so friendly it was hard to stay angry. "Agreed," he said.

"Good," said Eben. "Now we can be friends." He took his hand from Thomas's head. "Come on. I'll show you around. My family's been here for three days."

"How old are you?" Eben asked.

"I'll be eleven next month," Thomas answered.

"I'm nearly twelve," Eben told Thomas as they walked by the barracks. "Next month I can start training with the soldiers. I'd like to go with them when they fight the Tories. I can shoot as well as any man here. But they won't let you *really* fight until you are fourteen."

"I wish I had my gun," Thomas said bitterly. "Those Tories stole it. Even if we could go back, we don't have a weapon to protect us or to use for hunting. They killed our cow and stole our horse, too. Even if we are too young to fight, I wish there was something we could do."

They had walked nearly all the way around the fort. "This is where we get water," Eben said. He opened a small door and led the way down into a cool, dark tunnel. "There's a spring down here. The river is just a few feet away."

The door opened again and there was Emma,

hands on her hips. "I thought I saw you going in here. Mama says you are to come back right now."

"Tell Mama I'm coming," Thomas said.

"Mama says I am to bring you back with me," Emma insisted, much to Thomas's embarrassment.

Eben, however, only grinned. "I'll see you in the morning," he said.

Thomas followed Emma back to the barracks. "I can't find Abigail," Emma said. "She should have been here before us." Thomas knew she was thinking about the smoke they had seen that morning.

"Do you think she's dead?" Emma said softly.

"Naw," Thomas said, trying to sound as though he believed what he was saying. "Maybe they decided to keep going down the river."

"Do you think we'll ever get back home?" Emma asked suddenly.

Thomas shook his head. "Not much to go back to," he said gruffly. They walked the rest of the way in silence. People were settling down for the evening, but their faces were still tense and anxious. Thomas doubted that many would sleep well that night. It seemed odd, sleeping with so many strangers. Some were in their tents, but many more were squeezed into the barracks.

Someone, perhaps Mrs. Muldoon, had found a crate and a piece of quilt to make a bed for Ben. Emma had curled up next to their mother on their one cot, while Thomas tried to get comfortable on the hard wooden floor. One of the soldiers had given him a blanket, and he folded one corner of it, trying to make a pillow for his head. Even at night the fort was noisy, and it was a long time before he finally fell asleep.

The next morning he was stiff and sore. A woman offered the Bowdens each a biscuit and a steaming cup of coffee to share. They accepted gratefully, knowing most families had little enough for themselves.

More settlers arrived, among them Abigail Hailey and her parents. "Our boat sank," she said. "We went to one of the smaller forts across the river. But Father thought we would be safer here." Abigail was a skinny, pinched-faced girl who never sat still. Thomas did not like her much, but she was Emma's friend and he was interested in any news. So he listened carefully as she told of her escape. He thought about Mr. Hailey's *Gulliver's Travels,* now burned up with the rest of the Bowdens' belongings.

Shortly after breakfast gunshots were heard some distance from the fort. Soldiers paced the walkway, peering over the stockade walls, while people below called up anxiously, "Do you see anything?"

Thomas found Eben by the gate. "I heard two men were sent out before dawn on a spy mission," he said tersely. "They were supposed to find out if John Butler's army is really here." He pounded his fist into his other hand. "Why didn't they ask me? I know these woods better than anyone."

Suddenly there was shouting beyond the gate. "Open up. Open up."

Calling for Colonel Denison, the guards swung open the gates just wide enough to let two men stumble through. They sank to the ground in exhaustion.

"We ran into a patrol," one of them managed to gasp. "We barely escaped with our lives."

Colonel Denison's voice sagged with disappointment. "Rest for a moment and then give me your report," he said, turning back to his headquarters.

"Not much to report," the other man said bitterly. "We only made it about two miles. Didn't see anything except the six Tories and two Indians chasing us."

The men were led away and the crowd drifted apart. Eben had disappeared.

The day wore on, with people more uneasy than ever. Mrs. Muldoon had managed to bring a tiny supply of flour and dried apples with her. Thomas's mother helped her bake a few delicious pies in a small black Dutch oven. They traded these to the soldiers for some jerky and a few potatoes and onions. She shared the food with the Bowdens. "Something had better happen pretty soon," she confided to Mrs. Bowden. "Our food supplies are dangerously low."

Thomas sat down on the dusty ground and watched the militia drill. Nobbin sat beside him as though he too was curious. Officers from the Continental Army were teaching the militia and the settlers how to fight together like a real army. The men and older boys lined up in formation, leaving a space between each man. The first row stepped forward, knelt on one knee, and pretended to shoot. Then in turn the second and third rows stepped forward into the empty spaces while the first row of men reloaded. They did it over and over until every man kept in step.

Thomas wandered off to search for Eben, but it was hard to find anyone in the confusion. He wiped the sweat off his forehead. With so many people crowded into the fort, the dust and heat were almost unbearable. Tempers were short. Everywhere he went he saw groups of people arguing about what to do. Thomas stopped among a group of men gathered around Lazarus Stewart. He was urging people to fight. He said anyone who didn't was a coward. Others argued that Lazarus Stewart was brave but foolish, and that the people would be safe in the fort. "If Butler brought his army down the river on boats, they probably don't have any heavy artillery with them," one man argued. "Without big guns they will never be able to take this fort."

"They could just as well sit outside until we starve," Stewart retorted.

Thomas grew tired of listening. No one seemed to know what to do. He found his mother sitting on a crate in the shade of a spindly oak tree near the barns. She looked up at him and tried to smile. "Mrs. Muldoon is finishing the last of the pies," she said.

"Come and play tag with us," Emma said, running up and taking Thomas by the hand.

Thomas shook his head.

"Go on," urged his mother. "You need some fun. Next thing I know you will be growing a long white beard."

"Beard? Who has a beard?" Mrs. Muldoon plopped herself down on a crate next to Thomas's mother. "My first husband had a beard. It tickled when he kissed me," she added with a twinkle in her eye.

She handed Thomas and Emma a piece of warm apple pie wrapped up in a clean white cloth. "Better eat it before anyone sees you," she said cheerfully as they thanked her. "I make the best apple pie in the state."

Thomas took a juicy bite. It was delicious. He licked a drip off his finger, not wanting to waste the tiniest bit. He watched the younger children playing battle, using sticks as imaginary guns.

There were arguments over who would play the enemy. No one wanted to be a wicked Tory. Then you had to die almost immediately. Thomas wished he was young enough to join them. Somehow he didn't fit anywhere. He was too young to fight for real and too old to pretend.

He touched Emma's arm. "You're it," he yelled, racing away.

"No fair," Emma shouted, racing after him.

Thomas ducked behind some tents and circled back around to the cabins. Emma was running in the wrong direction. Thomas chuckled. Then suddenly he felt himself nearly flying through the air as someone jerked his arm and pulled him into a space between two cabins. "Don't make a sound," a voice whispered in his ear.

SEVEN

—•—

Eben's Plan

"Eben," Thomas blurted out, picking himself up.

"Shh." Eben peeked around the corner, making sure they were alone. Then he crouched down and drew a map in the dirt with a stick. "My house isn't too far from here. It's just up the road past Tuttle's mill. From there we would be around the bend in the river and could see more of the valley. If the Tory army is there, we're sure to find out. And if we come back with some information, we'll be heroes."

Thomas hesitated. "What makes you think we could make it when those other men couldn't?"

"I know every inch of land around there," Eben boasted. "I've got traplines all along the river. If we do get caught, we'll just say I was checking my traps. But we won't get caught," he added quickly at Thomas's look of alarm. He rocked back on his heels. "You said you wished we could do something to help."

Thomas hesitated. "How would we get out of the fort without being seen?" he asked.

"That's the easy part. I've done it before. The spring makes a little run into the river. You just hold your breath, duck under the water, and come up on the other side of the walls. We could get there and back in a couple of hours. No one would even miss us."

Slowly Thomas nodded.

"Meet me at the springhouse after dark," Eben said. He erased the map from the ground and ran off.

That evening Thomas had to make sure he didn't appear too eager to go to bed. He grumbled as usual when Mrs. Bowden announced it was time. He stretched out on his blanket, trying to keep his eyes open while he waited for the even breathing to tell him his mother slept. At last, when he was sure Emma and his mother both were asleep, he got up and tiptoed out the door and into the night.

"I thought you weren't coming," Eben whispered from the shadows of the springhouse.

"I had to make sure no one saw me," Thomas protested.

"I brought my gun," Eben said. "I found some oiled cloth to wrap it in to keep it dry. Take off your breeches. We'll wrap our clothes up, too."

Thomas peeled off his clothing. He shivered as the night air touched his skin.

Eben touched his arm. "Just hold your breath and dive down. Ready?"

Thomas nodded. Then he realized that Eben could not see him in the dark. "I'm ready," he said.

They felt their way into the springhouse. Thomas heard a splash and then silence. He slipped into the water, and holding his breath, he plunged in. The stream was not very deep, and Thomas's stomach scraped along the muddy bottom as he squeezed between the springhouse posts. He pushed himself forward by his elbows and toes until he was sure he'd cleared the walls of the fort. Then he climbed out of the water, shivering in the night air.

It was darker than he had expected. He could hear the river rushing by only a few feet away. A dark shape moved along the edge of the stream. "Get dressed," whispered Eben.

Thomas tugged on his clothes. Then, bending low in the tall grass, the boys made their way silently around the fort. "We'll make better time if we follow the road," Eben said. "It goes past the mill and then there's a little stone bridge. After that it's not too far to the Wintermoot fort. We can ask them what they've seen."

The road was little more than a heavily used trail creased with deep ruts, which made walking difficult. Thomas stepped quickly, grateful that clouds hid the moon. Even so, he imagined Indians behind every bush, and his heart beat with such a loud *thump! thump!* that he thought they must hear it back at the fort.

Tuttle's mill was still and dark, the big water-wheel silent and abandoned. Several nearby cabins had also been deserted. Eben pulled Thomas into the shadows at the stone bridge and spoke softly. "We haven't seen a sign of John Butler's army. Maybe there aren't any Tories here at all."

"There are Tories here, all right. They burned my house. Remember?" Thomas asked bitterly.

"You only saw a few soldiers," Eben reminded him. He stood up. "All right, let's go on to the Wintermoot fort." He stopped and turned back to Thomas. "If anything happens and we get separated, we'll meet back here at the mill. Agreed?"

Thomas nodded. "We'd better hurry. We've been gone a long time."

Eben started off again at a brisk walk. Thomas almost had to run to keep up. The only sounds were a few crickets and the night insects buzzing through the grass and, far away, the howl of a wolf.

Then Eben pulled at his arm. "Listen," he hissed. Thomas had heard it, too. It was the sound of many voices, though it was muffled and distant.

"What do you think we should do?" Thomas whispered.

"Keep going," Eben said, "but a mite more carefully."

The road was little more than a trail now, but by unspoken agreement they abandoned it for the high grass. The noise grew louder with each step. Soon they could smell smoke, and a red glow lit the sky.

When they reached the Wintermoot fort, it was

silhouetted in the glow of many campfires. Eben grabbed Thomas's arm and pulled him into the brush. "Do you see that?" he said furiously.

The gates to the fort were standing open. Even as they watched from their hidden lookout, two British officers in red coats came out of the fort and stood talking with two other men wearing Tory green.

"That traitor Wintermoot has turned over his fort. We need to get closer and hear what they're saying," Eben said.

Every part of Thomas wanted to run back to the safety of the Forty Fort. How could they have been so foolish as to think they could accomplish what grown men had not been able to do? But Eben was already wiggling closer, moving silently on his belly like a snake. Thomas reluctantly followed.

They climbed up a small hill and hid behind some bushes at the top. From here they had a plain view of the clearing around the fort. "There are so many," Thomas whispered.

Indeed, the whole clearing was crowded with men. In the fields there seemed to be some sort of headquarters. Beyond that, hundreds of soldiers, some in red and some in green, were setting up camp. A little further away Indian warriors had set up their own camp. They, too, seemed to number in the hundreds.

"We've got to get back and tell them," Thomas whispered. "There are far too many for our men to fight."

Eben nodded. Thomas slid backward over the trail they had just made. Eben turned to follow, but as he did, his foot kicked at a boulder perched at the top of the hill. There was a clatter of gravel as the large rock suddenly loosened and tumbled down into the clearing, bouncing several times before it came to a stop. Thomas heard a shout from one of the soldiers who had nearly been struck. "There's someone up there."

"Run," Eben hissed.

Thomas frantically scrambled away. Soldiers were clambering up the hill after them. He could hear their shouts and pounding feet. Thomas thought Eben was behind him, but he wasn't sure, and he couldn't risk calling his name to find out. He ran low to the ground and tried to stay as hidden as possible. At last, he reached the mill and squeezed behind the waterwheel. His breath came in short, jagged gasps as his heart slowly returned to normal. He could not hear the men following anymore. Maybe they had given up. The night was deathly quiet. "Eben?" he called softly.

There was no answer. Nor was there later when he called again. Finally he was forced to admit to himself that Eben had been captured.

EIGHT

A Daring Escape

It took nearly an hour for Thomas to make his way back to the Wintermoot fort. He circled around, avoiding the hill in case a guard had been stationed nearby. The camp was quiet now; many of the soldiers were rolled up in blankets asleep. Crouching in the grass, he gazed over the camp, looking for his friend. Finally he spotted him. Eben was sitting on the ground with his back to a tree at the edge of the camp. His arms had been forced behind him and his hands were tied together. Thomas made a wide circle, stopping directly behind the tree. He hid in a clump of bushes.

Two men squatted in front of Eben, questioning him. "I live near here. I was just checking my traplines," Thomas heard his friend say. His voice was dull, as though he'd repeated this story many times.

The men stood up. "Maybe he's telling the truth," one of them said.

"Doesn't matter," said the second. "We can't let him go now. Let's ask Butler what he wants to do with him. I need some sleep."

Thomas remained motionless until the men reached the gates of the fort and disappeared inside. Then he inched his way forward until he was directly behind the tree. "It's me," he whispered.

"You shouldn't be here," Eben whispered. "Get back to the fort. Warn them about the size of the army."

Thomas shook his head even though he knew Eben could not see him. "I'm not leaving you," he said stubbornly. "We'll go together."

"Well, then, hurry," Eben said. "The soldiers took my gun. But they don't know there is a knife in my boot. Reach in and get it so you can cut these ropes."

Thomas peered around the tree. In order to reach Eben's boot, he would have to step out into the open.

A twig snapped somewhere behind him. Before he could react, he felt himself yanked upward by his hair until he was on his knees. A knife blade glittered with a reflection from the fires as a hand was raised. It was only a matter of a second, yet it was enough time for Thomas to think of his mother. He felt more sad than afraid. He was going to die and he would never see her again.

"Stop!" The voice was stern, the voice of a man who was used to giving orders and being obeyed. The Indian warrior lowered the knife but did not release his hold on Thomas's hair.

"I don't want anyone killed until we give them a chance to surrender tomorrow." The officer was wearing a coat of bright green.

The Indian still did not release Thomas, and for a minute it seemed that the entire world had stopped. The officer, who might have been John Butler himself, stared at Thomas's capturer. At last, with a grunt of anger, the Indian thrust the boy away. Thomas landed on his face in the dirt beside Eben.

"I knew there were two of you," the officer

said mildly. "That's why we had a guard posted. I figured you'd come back to try to save your friend."

Thomas groaned. How could he have been so foolish? He had given up the chance to warn the Forty Fort and walked right into a trap.

"We'd better put you boys somewhere safe," the officer said. He unsheathed his sword and, with one quick slice, undid Eben's bonds.

Some of the sleeping soldiers were awake now, roused by the commotion. They watched as Thomas and Eben were escorted to a small shed inside the fort. The door was bolted.

"What do you think they will do to us?" Thomas asked Eben.

His friend rubbed his wrists. The ropes had made painful-looking burn marks. "Trade us for other prisoners, if we are lucky. Kill us if we're not," he answered shortly. "But I don't figure on waiting to find out."

Eben pulled the knife out of his boot, then slipped it in again quickly as the door opened. A soldier handed them a tin plate with two hard biscuits, some jerky, and two cups of strong black tea.

The boys sat, backs to the wall, and gratefully ate. It was nearly morning. Thomas imagined his mother rising and discovering that he was missing. His stomach knotted, knowing the pain and worry he had caused.

As if he read his thoughts, Eben smiled thinly. "If these Tories don't kill us, my papa will," he said.

"It was a bad idea," Thomas agreed.

"Not bad," Eben insisted. "We got the information we wanted, didn't we? All we have to do is get back and tell them."

The boys examined the walls of the shed. They were poorly made, and a glimmer of light showed through the chinks in the rotten wood. The shed's walls formed part of the outer walls of the fort. They would only have to cross a small clearing to reach the woods. Eben took his knife and started working on the boards.

Thomas kept watch through a space in the walls at the front of the shed. "There are three men on horses just riding out," he reported. "They are carrying white flags."

"They wouldn't be going to surrender," Eben said. "Not with an army this big."

"Maybe they're going to demand that the fort surrender," Thomas suggested.

Eben snorted. "My brother would never surrender and neither would the other soldiers." He went back to work.

Thomas watched through the crack as soldiers came and went. What chance did the Forty Fort have against so many? But he kept his thoughts to himself.

The boys worked steadily, each taking turns chipping away the wood while the other stood guard. It was harder than they thought at first, but by midmorning they had made a good-sized hole. Each piece they freed was carefully slipped back into place, to fool anyone who came in. No one came, though, and Thomas wondered if they had been forgotten.

Some time later a small number of men left the Wintermoot fort and headed in the direction of the Forty Fort. It was Thomas's watch, and he shook his head in amazement. Why was Butler sending out so few men? It was peculiar. The soldiers at the Forty Fort could easily defeat such a small army.

Most of the Indians headed across a grassy meadow and disappeared into the trees. For the first time that day Thomas felt hopeful. Maybe the Indians did not want to fight, after all.

"It's almost big enough to get through," Eben said.

"Let me take a turn." Thomas snatched up the knife and worked at a furious pace, chipping off enough wood to make a hole big enough to squeeze through.

"How are we going to get past the army?" Eben asked. "Even if we make it to the woods without being seen, the army is between us and the Forty Fort."

"The river," Thomas said. "Maybe we can find a boat." He pushed the loosened blocks of wood, jumping with dismay at the loud noise they made as they tumbled out. He stuck his head out the newly made opening, expecting a shout of discovery. When nothing happened, he wiggled free, with Eben right behind.

The two boys sprinted for the woods. Once they'd reached the shelter of the trees, Thomas looked back. Apparently their escape had not yet been discovered. Eben gave him a triumphant grin. "We made it."

"Not yet," Thomas said. "We still have to find a boat."

Walking as quietly as possible, they headed toward the river. The woods gave way to grassy shore, and Thomas breathed a sigh of relief. Two small boats were beached along the bank.

"Now we've made it," he said. No sooner had he spoken the words than from behind them came the sound of angry shouts.

"Hurry," Eben yelled, dashing for the nearest boat. "I think they just discovered that we escaped."

NINE

Out of Time

The boats were tied to stakes driven in the ground. Precious seconds were lost while Thomas fumbled frantically to untie one. The shouts were growing closer. While he worked, he was aware that Eben had run to the other boat. Thomas saw the flash of his knife, and the second boat was free. Eben pushed it into the water with a splash. It bobbed along, slowly drifting away from the shore. Eben ran toward Thomas, his knife ready, just as Thomas loosened the knot. "Now they can't follow us," Eben said.

The boys gave a mighty push and the boat slid smoothly into the water. At the last moment they leaped in and grabbed the oars.

The river was wide here. The first boat was caught in the swift current and moving away. They headed toward a small island with a thick growth of trees and brush. "Let's go around to the other side," Eben said. Paddling furiously, the boys guided the boat to the far side of the island and glided into the cover of the trees just as their pursuers reached the river. Thomas and Eben stayed quiet, hoping they hadn't been seen.

The men on shore cursed. There was a sharp *bang,* and Thomas felt a burning on his shoulder.

Eben pushed him down in the boat. "They are shooting through the trees," he whispered. Then in alarm he said, "You're bleeding."

Thomas looked at his shoulder. The bullet had torn a furrow in his shirt. A thin trickle of blood seeped onto the ragged edges. "It just scratched me," he said quietly.

On shore, someone was yelling at the man who had fired the shot. "Do you want to ruin the ambush? Get back in your positions."

"Not going to be much of an ambush if those boys get back and tell," the first man snarled.

"They don't know anything except that we're here. And Denison knows that by now."

"I hope you're right," the first man said as the voices moved away.

"What are they talking about?" Thomas asked. "What ambush?"

Eben seemed to understand right away. "Those Indians you saw weren't running away," he said angrily. "They'll be waiting in the woods."

Thomas paled. The men at the Forty Fort would be fooled by the small number of Tory soldiers into thinking they'd have a sure victory. Instead, they would be walking right into a trap.

The boat was riding the current. In a moment they would drift into sight. Eben used an oar to pole the boat back to the riverbank. Then he examined Thomas's wound. "It's not bad, but it's not good either. That's going to hurt some, I'll wager."

"It's going to hurt a lot," Thomas said grimly. "It already does. Come on. Let's get back to the fort."

The distance by river was not far. A short time later they rounded the bend and saw the Forty Fort straight ahead. Thomas thought of his mother while he rowed. By now she must be nearly beside herself with worry. Maybe she wouldn't be so unhappy with him when she heard what they had been able to learn.

As they guided the boat close to shore, Eben suddenly stopped rowing. "Why is it so quiet?" he asked anxiously.

Then from the direction of the mill came the jaunty sound of pipes playing. "You don't think they have already gone to fight, do you?" Eben said, voicing the fear that was in Thomas's mind.

"Hurry," Thomas said. Ignoring his aching shoulder, he rowed with all his might. At the fort the bank was too steep for them to disembark. They were forced to go to a dock a short distance away. In better times a man had run a small ferry there, rowing people across the river. It was deserted now, but two boats bobbed in the water, securely tied to the dock.

Taking only enough time to tie their boat next to the others, they raced the distance back to the fort.

As they approached the gates, they heard a volley of shots, muffled by distance but unmistakable. Thomas mentally counted off the drill he had watched the soldiers practice the day before. When he heard the second volley, sounding further away, he knew. "We're too late," he said tiredly. "It has already started."

Two old men opened the gate and the boys tumbled in. Thomas's shoulder was throbbing, but he was too unhappy to notice. The fort was much less crowded with the soldiers gone. The children were silent, too frightened for play, and the women stood in quiet groups, listening to the sounds of battle. Mrs. Bowden and Emma rushed up to them. Eben's mother was already scolding him in a loud voice.

Mrs. Bowden's eyes were swollen and red, but her voice was angry. "How could you have gone outside?" she said. "I thought you'd been killed. How could you do this to me? Do you think this is some kind of game?"

"They are walking into a trap." Thomas began to cry. "We wanted to save them, but we're too late."

"Who is walking into a trap?" One of the old soldiers grabbed Thomas by the arm.

"Somebody has to warn them," a woman wailed when Thomas and Eben told what they had overheard. She ran to the gate as though she would try herself, but another woman grabbed her arm. "It's too late," the second woman said. "If you go out there, you will be killed, too. Then who will care for your children?"

The first woman fell to the ground, sobbing. For a moment everyone in the fort was silent. They looked at one another, faces white with horror. Far away they heard gunfire, but it was no longer in even volleys. Instead, it was a steady roar like the sound of distant thunder on a hot summer afternoon.

"What happened to your arm?" Emma cried, looking at the blood-encrusted shirt.

Mrs. Bowden inspected the wound. "I'll see if Mrs. Muldoon has some salve for that," she said. The anger had fled from her voice, leaving it tired and wooden.

Thomas followed her back to the barracks and sat outside with Nobbin while Mrs. Muldoon helped her tear some bandages from a clean white apron.

Mrs. Muldoon handed him a biscuit, and Thomas greedily stuffed it into his mouth. "I was going to make some johnnycakes, but there is hardly any cornmeal left. Our food stores are getting mighty thin." Mrs. Muldoon's usual smile was missing.

Emma was listening intently to the gunfire. "What do you think is happening?" Emma said.

"They are fighting," Thomas snapped. "Can't you hear?"

"What will happen to us if they lose?"

"I don't know," Thomas admitted in a gentler voice.

Emma touched her hair. "Some people are saying if the Indians come they will scalp everyone."

Mrs. Bowden overheard Emma's whispered worry. She knelt beside them in the dust and gathered them to her. "The Tory leaders sent soldiers with a white flag. They promised to let us go in peace if we surrender."

"Do you believe them?" Thomas asked. His eyes met his mother's over the top of Emma's head.

"We have to believe them," Mrs. Bowden answered. Her voice was steady, but Thomas saw the doubt in her eyes.

Mrs. Bowden motioned for Thomas and Emma to follow her inside. Ben was sound asleep in his makeshift cradle.

"From now on I want us all to stay very close together," she said, with a stern look at Thomas. "As soon as we have the chance, I'm going to take us all to my sister's house in Philadelphia. If we can get down the river to Harrisburg, I'm sure we can hire a wagon to take us there. The last I heard, your father was nearby, and I know my sister will take us in."

Mrs. Bowden paused. "Rachel is one of those who has remained loyal to King George."

"You mean she's a Tory?" Thomas was horrified.

"Perhaps she has changed her mind by now," Mrs. Bowden answered. "Tory or no, she will take us in. We are family."

Thomas crossed his arms defiantly. "I won't live with Tories. Wouldn't be right, our father fighting against them and all."

It had been four years since Thomas had seen Aunt Rachel. Uncle Charles was a merchant, and their house was a fine brick house with three stories. Thomas remembered that Aunt Rachel was pretty and kind. It was hard to think of her as the enemy.

"We have noplace else to go," Mrs. Bowden reminded him. "And you will take your sister and

Ben there if anything should happen to me. Promise me."

"Don't say that," Emma cried. "Nothing will happen to you."

Mrs. Bowden brushed away her tears. "I certainly hope not. But just in case, I want you to know my plan. Your father would know to look for you there after this horrible war is over."

Numbly Thomas nodded. Mrs. Bowden picked up the hem of her skirt. Thomas's eyes widened at the sight of the sewing. Usually his mother's stitches were even and straight. This thread had been carelessly looped over and over. "That last night at home I sewed some coins into my hem," she explained. "It was dark," she said with a rueful look at the messy stitches. "There are more in Ben's blanket."

Mrs. Bowden picked up Ben to feed him, and Thomas and Emma wandered back outside. By now even the small children sat quietly, subdued by their mothers' worried looks.

Suddenly a cry went up from the gates. "Somebody's coming," a guard shouted.

A minute of silence passed. "Is it one of ours?" a woman called out fearfully.

There was another long minute until the guard replied. "It's our men. Open the gates."

The gate swung open. Several men stumbled through. "It was a trap," one of them shouted. His eyes were wild with fear and his clothes bloody. One of his arms hung uselessly at his side. "The Tories kept falling back. We thought we were winning. But Indians were hiding in the woods and they surrounded us."

A woman sank to the ground with a long, mournful wail. Others crowded around, seeking news of husbands, fathers, and brothers. For the first time Thomas was glad that his father had not been with them. Again and again the gates were opened to let in a pitiful few survivors, most of them wounded. "It was horrible," one of the men sobbed. "Hardly anyone survived, and the captured men are being tortured and scalped."

Mrs. Bowden and Abigail's mother ripped clean white aprons into bandages and tended to the wounded soldiers. Mr. Hailey had left with the militia, but he had not returned. Colonel Denison galloped back to the fort, but only a few soldiers were with him. As darkness fell, it was plain no more would return. From outside the gates came the sound of war whoops, and then they heard terrible screams. Emma sat on the ground, rocking herself back and forth. Mrs. Bowden stooped and held her hands over Emma's ears. Nobbin put his head in Emma's lap and whined softly.

When the colonel walked to the open area in the middle of the fort, the women gathered their children together and slowly formed a circle around him.

Thomas and Emma stood with their mother. Ben yawned in her arms. Emma tickled him and was rewarded with a smile.

"We've lost too many men today to defend the fort," the colonel said with a heavy voice. "The enemy is celebrating their victory. But soon they will come here, and when they do, we will have no choice but to surrender."

TEN

—◆—

A Desperate Decision

In the stunned silence that followed, Thomas stepped forward. "Sir, why don't we try to escape? There are still some boats by the ferry dock. I saw them this morning."

There was a buzz of conversation. Colonel Denison held up his hand. "If the boy is right, we can use this time to ferry you across the river. The other side seems safe enough. You can try to make your way to one of the forts down the river or walk east across the mountains. You may have a better chance either way than if you stay here. My men will defend this fort as long as we can, to give you time to get away."

The women pressed close, pounding him with

questions. Wearily the colonel waved them away. "You will have to make your own decisions. But hurry. The enemy could be here at any second."

The colonel walked away, his shoulders slumped in despair.

Mrs. Bowden's decision was made quickly. "Are you sure about the boats?" she asked Thomas.

"I saw them," Thomas repeated.

Mrs. Bowden looked at the sky. It was tinged red with the glow of many fires scattered throughout the valley. "We'll take our chances on the mountains rather than trust men like that for mercy." Gathering up the baby, she pushed her family through the crowd gathering by the gates. Two soldiers were dividing people into groups. "Move quietly," one of them said in a soft voice. "We will row you across."

Wide-eyed, Emma looked all around. "Where is Abigail?" she wailed to Mrs. Bowden, but the Haileys were nowhere to be found.

"When everyone is across the river, some of us are going to take one of the boats downstream," said a woman.

Thomas glanced at his mother. Her face was

pale, but her lips were pressed together in determination. With her fear of boats, just crossing the river was going to be an ordeal for her.

"There are rapids to get through, and who knows if some of the Tories are downriver. We're going to head across the mountains," said someone else.

Still another woman had a warning. "There's a terrible swamp to cross before you get to the mountains. If you get past that, there are three paths over the mountains, but how would you find them in the dark?"

Eben slipped through the crowd to Thomas. "My mother is staying. She won't leave until we find out what happened to my brother. She doesn't believe the Tories will kill women and children."

Thomas saw the fear in his eyes. He grasped his hand. "Maybe we will see each other again."

"Good-bye, my friend," Eben said gravely, just as the crowd pushed him away.

Mrs. Muldoon found them in line. She gave Thomas's mother a big hug and slipped a package in her apron pocket. "You are not coming?" Mrs. Bowden asked.

Mrs. Muldoon shook her head. "I'm too old to walk across the mountains. I think I will take my chances staying here."

A child cried out. "You must keep the babies quiet," the soldier warned.

Emma looked around frantically. "Nobbin. What about Nobbin?"

Hearing his name, Nobbin wiggled through the crowd and sat down quietly beside Emma's feet. The soldier frowned. "We can't take the dog."

"We can't leave him," Emma cried. "He came all this way with us. We have to take him."

"He will have to stay behind," Mrs. Bowden said sadly. "The boats will be too full."

"Don't worry," said Mrs. Muldoon. "I'll keep him with me." She patted Nobbin's head as she spoke.

Another soldier, with dried blood on his bandaged head, slipped out of the gates. A minute later he was back. "I think it's safe," he announced in a hoarse whisper. "I walked all the way to the river and saw no one."

Slowly the gates were opened just enough for the women and children to slip through. "Hurry," the soldiers urged them quietly.

"Stay," Thomas told Nobbin, choking back a sob. Obediently Nobbin sat, looking at Thomas with sad brown eyes. Thomas forced himself to look away. Emma gave him a last pat, tears streaming down her face.

"Keep close," Mrs. Bowden had time to whisper. Then the waiting crowd pushed forward and suddenly Thomas found himself outside the gates.

It was lighter than Thomas had expected. The horizon glowed with an eerie red from the many fires, and in the distance he could hear faint shouts, screams of the tortured captives, and the sound of occasional gunfire. But close to the fort it was silent except for the gentle lap of water along the shore. It was a warm night, but Thomas shivered with excitement and fear. He held Emma's hand so he wouldn't lose her in the dark. He could feel her trembling, and her palm was damp. Hardly daring to breathe, the group pressed close to the fort walls and inched their way toward the water. Thomas and Emma walked silently beside their mother, gasping with relief when they reached the boats.

"Quickly now," the soldiers whispered as they

clambered aboard. One soldier took his place to row while a second man gave them a shove, then jumped in as the boat started to move. He cradled his gun as he faced the far shore, alert to any suspicious movement.

The boats glided swiftly across the river. Thomas stared at the shoreline, barely visible in the moonlight. Could they really have escaped so easily?

Just when he had begun to believe they were going to make it, he heard a loud splash. His breath caught in his throat, and he twisted in his seat, expecting to see dark warriors slipping over the banks. Then he almost laughed when he saw a fat black shape paddling furiously, trying to keep up. "It's Nobbin," Emma whispered. "He must have gotten away from Mrs. Muldoon."

The soldier at the back of the boat leaned over the edge. Thomas could not see what he was doing. Thomas could no longer see Nobbin either, and he feared the faithful dog would be swept away in the swift current and drowned. Then the soldier sat back up, and Thomas could see his grin in the moonlight. He pointed down in the water. Somehow he had managed to fasten the mooring rope

around Nobbin's belly. Nobbin's legs churned the water. With the rope anchoring him safely to the boat, he actually made progress, swimming until he had drawn up beside them. Thomas tapped Emma so she could see. As the boat bumped onto the shore, the soldier loosened the rope and Nobbin climbed out of the water. He happily shook himself dry, spraying water over everyone.

One of the women stepped aside, glaring at the soldier who had saved Nobbin. "That dog will endanger us all," she hissed. "You should not have risked our lives to save a dog."

"These children have lost everything. No need to add their dog to the list." To Thomas he whispered, "Can you keep him quiet?"

"Yes, sir," Thomas said.

The soldier nodded. Ignoring the woman, he said to the other passengers, "Walk away from the shore so you won't be seen." He jumped back in the boat. Then he and the other soldier pushed themselves away from the bank with an oar, heading back for another load of refugees.

The woman was still grumbling quietly about Nobbin. "She's right," said someone else. "The dog should stay behind. The small baby is danger enough."

"He would only follow us," Mrs. Bowden said.

"Then kill it," came a harsh answer.

Emma gasped, but Mrs. Bowden shook her head. "I will not. My children and I will go by ourselves. Then we will not be a danger to you."

She led them to a row of trees a few feet away from the water. It was darker there. The trees cast a heavy shadow and the moon had chosen that moment to hide behind the clouds. Thomas relaxed a little. He felt sure they would not be able to be seen from the opposite shore. He was aware of other people around him, but so silent was their passage that he could not be sure how many there were. Thomas concentrated on every footfall, making sure he did not step on branches. He glanced across the river. Shadowy figures slipped along the banks. In the distance was the muffled sound of gunfire. Sadness rushed over him, knowing this would be his last memory of the beautiful valley that had been his home. He forced his eyes away and marched determinedly toward the east.

ELEVEN

Into the Wilderness

Finally Mrs. Bowden halted for a few minutes' rest. They sat, huddled together on the damp earth, while she nursed Ben. Nobbin sat quietly beside them with his head on Emma's lap.

"It will be a hard walk over the mountains," Mrs. Bowden said. "We are strong, though, and I think we can make it."

"Why was that woman so mean about Nobbin?" Emma asked.

"She's afraid," Mrs. Bowden answered. "I talked to her at the fort, and she is a very nice lady. And she is right. Nobbin could put us in danger, if he should bark at the wrong time."

"He won't bark," Thomas said fiercely. "I won't let him."

Their mother gave them each a brief hug. "I don't see that we have much choice. Nobbin seems determined to come with us."

Mrs. Bowden stood up. "We need to get further away, and then we'll look for a place to sleep." As the faint sounds of the other refugees faded in the distance, Thomas took the lead.

"What if we get lost?" asked Emma, always the worrier.

Thomas pointed to a star, brighter than the others. "Father taught me how to find that star," he told her as they started walking. "He called it the North Star. With it we can always tell our direction. We want to go east, so that would be to the right of us when we are facing the star. In the daytime, we'll travel by the sun. It rises in the east and sets in the west."

A wolf howled somewhere off in the distant hills as they stumbled through the unfamiliar forest. Although the moon gave off some light, it did not reach the ground through the thick canopy of trees. Several times they heard the crashing of something large passing nearby. It might have been another family like themselves, but they dared not call out to see.

It was difficult to tell how much progress they were making. The ground was wet, with the mucky smell of swamp and the whining buzz of gollynippers. Mrs. Bowden covered the baby's face with his blanket, and Thomas broke off several low-growing pine branches to wave around as they walked. Even so, Thomas felt tiny stings as the insects landed on his arms and legs.

Thomas walked as fast as he dared. He tried to keep moving in the right direction, but it was difficult because the trees hid the stars from his view.

After several hours they came to a meadow, where the ground seemed drier. Several boulders stood out in the moonlight, making an open, cave-like space in between.

"Maybe we should rest for a while," he suggested. "The rocks might hide us if anyone comes."

"Do you think we are far enough away?" Mrs. Bowden asked.

Thomas stood perfectly still, listening. A chorus of frogs sang from somewhere close by. Crickets chirped a song of their own and a gentle breeze rustled the grass. It seemed like the most peaceful of summer nights.

"I don't know," he answered. "Do you think we should go on?"

His mother hesitated. "No, let's rest until morning. At least then we can see where we are going."

She handed the baby to Thomas while she picked handfuls of grass. Nobbin ran around the rocks, snuffing excitedly. He ran back to the family and softly whined. Thomas gave him a sharp tap on his nose. "Sit, Nobbin," he said.

Nobbin gave a soft yelp of surprise. But he sat quietly while Mrs. Bowden piled the grass in the narrow space between the rocks, making a fragrant bed. If they lay close to one another, there was just enough room for them all to stretch out. Mrs. Bowden kept Ben close to her. Nobbin slithered in between Thomas and Emma, but he seemed nervous, sniffing the air and wiggling about in the tiny space.

"Nobbin, sit," Thomas scolded sharply. There were so many dangers ahead that Thomas could not imagine how they could survive. His stomach was already empty and rumbling. It would take days to cross the mountains. Even if they had managed to escape John Butler's army, they still had to face wild animals and hunger. He told himself he should stay awake, but his eyelids were heavy. From Emma's steady breathing he guessed she was asleep, but he knew his mother was holding herself awake, listening, as he was. Finally he allowed himself to relax and soon he had drifted off to sleep.

The sun shining on his face woke him up a few short hours later. Before Thomas had even opened his eyes, he became aware that Nobbin was growling, a low rumble that warned of danger. At the same instant he heard his mother.

"Thomas. Thomas." His mother's voice was low but urgent. "Wake up. But don't move."

Thomas opened his eyes. He was on his back. It was light outside, just barely daybreak.

"Don't move," his mother's voice warned again.

He tried to see her without moving his head. She was sitting up, leaning against the largest boulder. She looked tired, and Thomas wondered if she had slept at all. She was staring at the boulder next to Thomas with an expression of horror.

"Snakes," she whispered. "Behind you. Don't move."

Thomas fought the urge to jump up screaming. Now he could feel something, something large, sliding close to his leg. Then it stopped and raised its head as though sensing danger. Thomas could see the copper color and hourglass pattern on its back. He bit his lips to keep from moaning.

The snake slid across Thomas's leg. Beads of sweat appeared on his forehead, and he tried to remember what his father had told him about copperheads. Last spring they had found a whole nest of them in a field they were plowing. "Copperheads are poisonous," Father had said. "The bite is painful, but most people won't die."

He moved his head ever so slightly to look at his mother. She was holding Nobbin. The dog was straining to get up, but Mrs. Bowden had him firmly pinned down.

Next to her, Emma was holding Ben, and her eyes were wide with shock. The snake had slid away.

"There may be more," Thomas whispered quietly.

Mrs. Bowden nodded. Without turning around, she said, "Emma, stand up slowly, put Ben on the boulder, and see if you can climb up beside him. Move very carefully and quietly."

Moving cautiously, Emma did as her mother said. The rock was somewhat flat on the top and low enough for her to reach up and place Ben there. Then, hanging on by her fingertips, she tried to boost herself up next to him. "I can't get up there," she whispered. "It's too high."

"Try standing on my back," Mrs. Bowden suggested quietly, never taking her eyes off the spot where the snake had first appeared beside Thomas.

After a few tries, Emma managed to boost herself to the rock. "I'm here, Mama," she said.

Mrs. Bowden looked at Thomas. "I think the snake came out of a hole under the rock behind you. I am going to climb up on the rock. Then I will grab your arm and pull you up as fast as I can. Do you understand?"

"Yes," Thomas whispered.

Slowly Mrs. Bowden stood. She scrambled to the top of the rock. Thomas almost smiled to see his usually sedate mother climbing rocks like a child. She sat down with her feet dangling over the edge. "Now slowly raise your arms," she said.

Thomas carefully raised his arms until they were only a few inches from his mother's hands.

"I'll count to three," Mrs. Bowden said. "Then you give yourself a boost and I will pull."

Thomas felt a tiny movement behind his leg. "Wait," he whispered. "I think there's another one."

His mother nodded. "I can see it now. They must be coming out to lie in the sun. We'll wait until it's gone." Thomas felt his fingertips grow numb, held above his head. He wasn't sure how much longer he could stay still in this position. By some miracle Nobbin was still, as though he understood the danger. Then, just before Thomas felt he could not stay frozen another second, his mother reached down and grasped his wrists. "One, two, three," she said quickly. At the same time he felt himself jerked into the air. His knees hit the side of the boulder, and he pushed himself upward. Out of the corner of his eye he saw a third snake, this one even larger than the others, slither after him. Then, like an angry whirlwind, Nobbin was there, lunging at the snake, jaws snapping, giving Thomas a chance to swing himself up. With a hiss, the snake swung toward the dog. Thomas sprawled on his stomach across the rock and, with one superhuman lunge, grabbed Nobbin by the scruff of his neck, pulling him up just as the snake struck the empty air where Nobbin had been a split second before. The snake coiled, as though confused; then it too slithered out from the rocks and disappeared from sight in the tall grass.

Thomas lay gasping for breath while Nobbin licked his face, his tail wagging, not knowing how close they had come to death. Emma was cheering, forgetting to be quiet. "You did it. You did it."

Mrs. Bowden hugged him. There were tears in her eyes, but she was grinning. "Are you all right?"

She had accidentally squeezed his sore shoulder, but Thomas assured her that he was unhurt. They looked down at the spot where he'd been only a few minutes before. In a hollow depression beneath the boulder they could see several more writhing bodies, disturbed by the sudden movement.

His mother watched them for several minutes. "I think we will make camp from now on while it is still light enough to see our sleeping companions," she said calmly.

"Nobbin was trying to tell us that something was wrong last night," Thomas said. "That's why he was whining."

Thomas couldn't help thinking of the dangers they still had to face. There were bears in these woods, and wolves. In addition to that, the hills were laced with Indian paths.

They found a small pond nearby. Mrs. Bowden washed Ben's diaper and spread it over a bush to dry while she took out a clean one from the small purse she had tied around her waist and put it on him. Thomas and Emma found a few ripe blackberries. The package from Mrs. Muldoon contained bread and cheese. Mrs. Bowden broke off a small piece for each of them. It tasted delicious, but Thomas was still hungry when they were done.

Thomas studied his mother while they ate.

"What are you thinking?" she asked.

"Remember that Indian woman we saw in the woods one day?" Thomas asked.

"I remember," said his mother. "She was gathering berries. I think we startled her as much as she startled us."

"I was thinking about how she carried her baby. He was strapped to her back. I thought that was a good idea. That way her arms didn't get so tired," Thomas said thoughtfully.

Mrs. Bowden nodded. "You're right. My apron," she said. "I think we could use it." She put the remaining bread and cheese in the purse and took off her apron. After several tries, Thomas managed to tie it into a pouch for the baby. The apron strings went over his mother's shoulders and tied beneath the baby's bottom. He lifted Ben inside.

"This is wonderful," said Mrs. Bowden. "The baby seems like hardly any weight at all this way."

Thomas looked at the mountains looming in front of them. Mrs. Bowden stood quietly behind him. "Do you think we can make it?" she asked in a low voice. The lightness of the last few minutes was gone as the reality of their situation came crashing down on them. "Maybe we should have followed the river. It was a hard decision to make by myself."

Mr. Bowden, who always made decisions very quickly, often teased his wife about how long it took her to make up her mind. "I make a list," she used to say. "All the good things on one side and all the bad on the other."

With the mountains stretching before them, Thomas realized a list wouldn't work this time. He couldn't think of a single thing to put on the good side. Whichever way they went, they were in terrible danger.

He knew what his mother needed to hear, even though he wasn't sure he believed it himself. "We can make it."

As they started, Emma walked beside him. "Do you remember Philadelphia?" she asked. Emma had been only five when they had loaded the wagon for the trip over the mountains to the valley.

"Not very well," he admitted. "The houses are real close together. And there are a lot of carriages and wagons going down the street. Mama says we'll be able to go to school there."

Emma did not look overjoyed at the thought of school without Abigail.

They walked in silence after that, saving their energy. At first the walk was easy. They pushed their way through a level valley with grasses nearly up to their waists. It was warm, and little trickles of sweat ran down Thomas's back. Once they thought they heard voices, but too far away to tell if they belonged to other refugees like themselves or Indians. Thomas grabbed Nobbin and they ducked down in the grass until the voices faded away.

After a few miles the land became wetter, and the mud sucked at their shoes, making it harder to walk. The trees grew so close together that little light could reach the ground, making it dismal and dark.

"I don't like it here," Emma said.

Thomas tipped back his head, trying to see the sky. "That's just because the trees are so tall." Thomas marveled at the soaring pines and hemlock growing so close together that they nearly blocked out the sun. "I wonder *why* these trees grew so tall here."

Mrs. Bowden forgot her worries long enough to smile at him. "Why Bowden, is there nothing that stops your curiosity?"

It seemed like a hundred years since his mother had used that nickname. So much had happened that the farm seemed like part of another life.

"I'm hungry already," Emma complained. "I wish I had something to eat."

"We must save what little food we have," her mother answered.

Thomas kicked at the soft earth with his toe, uncovering a fat worm. "We might get so hungry we have to eat worms," he teased.

Emma shivered. "I would rather starve."

Thomas shrugged, still teasing. "They are not so bad. I tasted one once."

"Liar," Emma said.

"Frogs!" Thomas said suddenly. "We could catch some frogs to eat. Of course," he added with a grin, "we would have to eat them raw."

Emma made a face at him. Then she smiled. "I guess I should thank you. I'm not hungry anymore."

TWELVE

———◆———

Across the Swamp

By late afternoon they were deep into the swamp. Each step was uncertain. Would the ground be firm, or would they sink into ankle-deep muck? Thomas was miserable. His shoulder ached, and the heat was nearly unbearable. The smell of rotting vegetation hung heavy in the air. Nobbin plodded silently beside them, sometimes in water that nearly covered his back. Dragonflies skittered across little pools, but the Bowdens were too miserable to enjoy the sight. Once, pushing through tall grass, they startled some long-legged birds into a noisy flight. Nobbin barked at them, but Thomas was too weary even to scold.

Emma gasped with delight as the birds rose

gracefully in the air. "What kind of birds are those, Mama?" she asked.

Mrs. Bowden wiped a splash of mud from her face with the sleeve of her dress. "I've got bigger things to worry about," she snapped. Thomas looked at his mother in surprise. It was not like her to be so cross. He knew why she was worried. Before many hours had passed, it would be nightfall. They would not find a place to sleep safely here, and yet there seemed to be no end to this dreadful swamp. There was no way for Mrs. Bowden to tend to Ben, and he wailed his misery, bouncing along on his mother's back. Thomas tried to set a faster pace, but it was impossible. They stumbled and fell in the slippery mud. Their clothes and hands were streaked with dirt.

The worst, though, was the hunger. Thomas's stomach ached with emptiness, and his head felt light. He found himself dreaming of food as he walked, his mother's good stew with vegetables from the garden and corn bread with butter. He thought so hard about the pie Mrs. Muldoon had given him he could almost taste it—the apples juicy and sweet, the crust so chewy.

He played a game with Emma, each of them trying to think of a more delicious meal.

"Turkey," Emma said. "Remember when Father went hunting and brought one home?"

Thomas nodded. His mother had roasted it on a spit in the fireplace, turning it often so that it was a deep golden brown.

He had been so intent on his thoughts that he was startled to notice they were almost out of the swamp. Ahead of them was a hill covered with a thick pine forest, and Thomas hurried, knowing that the higher ground would bring an end to the water and mud.

Suddenly Emma wailed, "My shoes are gone," and held up a foot caked with mud as proof.

Mrs. Bowden seemed almost ready to cry herself. "How could you be so careless?" she cried.

"I didn't even feel it," Emma said. "My feet were so muddy and wet I couldn't tell."

Thomas stopped. "Shall I go back and look?" he asked.

Mrs. Bowden hesitated. Then she shook her head. "Emma doesn't know when she lost them. It could have been hours ago."

"I'll share my shoes," Thomas said. "We can take turns wearing them."

They stumbled along in silence. They were climbing now, and the mountains, thickly forested and impossibly tall, stood before them. At last they came to a small lake with cool, clean water. They plunged in, washing away the mud and sweat and smiling once more.

Then Mrs. Bowden's smile froze, and she stared at Emma's bare feet. Something small and fat was clinging to her skin.

"Leeches!" Emma screamed. "Get them off of me—get them off."

Mrs. Bowden made Emma sit on the edge of the lake while she picked the leeches off one by one. "Thomas, go behind that tree and check yourself," she ordered.

Thomas did as he was told. When he removed his pants, he found several had attached themselves to his legs. He hadn't even felt them. He pulled them off and savored crushing them one by one with a stone. He and Emma waited while their mother detached several from herself and checked Ben, who luckily had none. Thomas pulled some from Nobbin, and the old dog licked his hand in thanks.

They did not dare waste any more daylight hours. Even before their clothes had dried, they set off again. They had left the soft mud of the swamp behind and were climbing steadily now. Even though there were three well-used trails across the mountains, they had not found any sign of them. Thomas knew they were heading in the right direction. Behind them the sun was low on the horizon, and the evening sky was streaked with red. Mrs. Bowden called a halt while she wrapped strips torn from her petticoat around Emma's feet for some protection from the rocky ground.

Thomas had a sudden idea. He gathered handfuls of grasses and stuffed them in the wrappings, making a soft padding for the bottoms of Emma's feet.

Mrs. Bowden smiled as Emma tried on her new grass shoes. "I can hardly feel the rocks," Emma announced.

Thomas's legs ached, but the only time they stopped again was to eat some blackberries they found growing at the edge of the forest. They stuffed their mouths full, but it did little to relieve the hunger.

Nobbin plodded along beside them. Both Emma and Thomas worried about him. At least they could eat blackberries and perhaps even some greens they found along the way, but there was nothing for their dog.

For a time they followed a small stream; then Mrs. Bowden sank to the ground and Thomas lifted the hot, cranky baby from her back. She looked at the setting sun with an anxious frown. "We've got to find some kind of shelter," she said.

"Emma and I will look," Thomas said. "Maybe we'll find something to eat, too."

"Don't go far," his mother said. She wet her skirt in the stream and wiped the baby's face.

Nobbin waded into the water to cool off. A minute later Thomas grinned and nudged Emma. Nobbin was lying on the muddy bank, happily devouring a large frog. "Raw," Thomas teased.

Emma looked sick and wouldn't watch, but Thomas knew she was glad Nobbin could find food for himself.

Emma was the one who finally found the perfect

spot. It was a cave, comfortable enough for the four of them to squeeze into. "Look for snakes," Emma demanded before she entered.

Thomas poked around with a stick, but the cave was empty. He was more worried about wild animals. He gathered rocks until it was too dark to see. With Emma's help, he piled the rocks in front of the entrance, leaving a little space at the top for air.

Mrs. Bowden passed out the remaining bread and cheese. There was barely a bite for each of them. Thomas chewed slowly, making it last.

"There are rocks poking me," Emma grumbled.

"There are rocks poking everyone," Thomas retorted. "Do you want to sleep out there?" He jerked his head toward the entrance.

"I want to be home. In my own bed," Emma grumbled.

"Stop acting like a baby," Thomas said. "You don't even have a bed anymore. Or a home. We're never going back again. Never!"

Emma glared at him. "You are just plain mean, Thomas," she shouted.

"That's better than being a whiny baby," Thomas hollered back.

"Thomas! Emma!" Mrs. Bowden put her arms around them both. There were tears in her eyes. "I need you both to be strong. Don't fight. If we don't stay close and work together, we will not survive."

Thomas sat down, his head hanging in shame. His mother was counting on him and he was acting like a spoiled child. It wasn't fair to Emma either. All day she had kept the pace, the last few hours walking without real shoes. And never once had she complained. Even now she was only saying the same things he was thinking. He thought of a riddle to cheer her up.

"Why does the miller wear a white hat?" he said.

"I don't know," Emma said crossly. For a minute Thomas thought his peace offering was not going to work. Then Emma sat down beside him. "So everyone knows he's the miller?"

Thomas shook his head. "To cover his head," he said with a chuckle.

"That's silly," Emma said, but she was smiling now. "A girl at the fort told me one. When is a boy not a boy?"

Thomas thought. "When he's a man!" he crowed.

"Wrong," laughed Emma. "It's when he's abed."

Mrs. Bowden laughed. Suddenly the tension was gone, and they were a family again. "That's just where we should be," she said.

Thomas stretched out on the rocky cave floor. "How can we get comfortable?" he mumbled. "Now that's a real riddle."

Mrs. Bowden sat up, leaning against a rocky wall. Thomas and Emma used her lap for a pillow, one on either side. The hunger was an actual pain in his stomach now, and Thomas tried not to think about food. The only one who seemed contented was Ben. Freed from his apron sling, he waved his chubby fists and feet in the air, gurgling to himself. Nobbin curled next to the baby, like a furry soldier, protecting him.

THIRTEEN

―――•――――

Hunger!

Thomas spent a fitful night, his sleep interrupted by unhappy dreams and his stomach rumbling with hunger. By the time he awoke, bruised and sore from his rocky bed, Thomas's stomach was screaming to be fed. When he stood up, he had to balance himself against the walls of the cave until the dizziness passed. Emma's face was pale, and she seemed to have hardly enough energy to stand up on wobbly legs.

"You wear the shoes today," Thomas said, handing them to her.

"I still don't think I can walk," she mumbled, as he put them on her feet. "I'm too weak."

Thomas forced himself to ignore the pain in his

middle. "Of course you can. Every step brings you that much closer to food. Mama says there is a settlement on the other side of the mountains. If we can find it, we'll find food and shelter. Mama says there is even an inn."

"If we can find it," Emma said.

"We will find it. Tomorrow," Thomas said, trying to convince himself as well as Emma. "Or maybe the next day."

Thomas pushed away the rocks from the entrance and stepped out of the cave. The sky was overcast and gloomy, the air humid and still. He sat down and wrapped his own feet, making a grass padding as he had done for Emma. Mrs. Bowden followed him out and stretched. She seemed pale and listless and hardly spoke as they tied Ben back into his pouch and started off. The way was steep, and their muscles soon ached with the effort. By nighttime they sank to rest beneath some trees, too exhausted to search for better shelter. Sometime after dark, thunder rolled in the distance and a hard rain fell.

Thomas tried to make a lean-to with some fallen pine branches, but it did little to stop rain from soaking them through. They started off again as soon as it was light, damp and too miserable to talk.

The next three days passed in a blur, one step following another. They would circle a high hill, hoping to find a passage through the mountainous terrain, but instead would face yet another hill. "Maybe we are lost," Emma cried.

"As long as we keep going east, we'll make it," Thomas said. "Tomorrow look at the sun. It always comes up in the east." In a marshy spot, they found a patch of tiny blueberries. They were delicious and sweet but did little to ease their hunger.

That night found them halfway up a steep hill, with no real shelter. They sank down, exhausted, and slept. During the night, Thomas awoke to the howling of wolves. They sounded close by, but Thomas could not bring himself to care. Beside him Nobbin whined and stirred restlessly. He heard his mother's quiet voice and knew that she had been awakened, too. "Stay, Nobbin," she whispered.

As soon as it was dawn, they started walking again. At noon they paused for a few minutes' rest, and Thomas, who was wearing the shoes, offered them to Emma. "I'm all right," Emma said.

Mrs. Bowden replaced the ragged strips around

Emma's feet with fresh ones. "We'd better get there soon," she joked weakly. "I'm running out of petticoat."

Later that afternoon Nobbin suddenly stopped and growled deep in his throat. Thomas caught a glimpse of gray fur flashing behind a tree. He pointed silently. "Wolves," he said flatly.

Mrs. Bowden tore the remaining bit of petticoat skirt. She tied it around Nobbin and handed the end to Thomas. "Hang on to him," she said. "If he tangles with the wolves, they'll kill him."

Thomas held his head. He felt strange and dizzy. If it were not for the wolves, he doubted he could go on. He knew they were waiting until the Bowdens were too weak to fight. So he plodded along, concentrating on one footfall after another.

"Are the wolves going to attack us?" Emma asked, with a worried look over her shoulder.

Mrs. Bowden shook her head. "I don't think wolves usually attack people. I think we need to find a really protected place to spend the night, though."

Thomas, who was in the lead, suddenly halted. "Oh no," he groaned.

Mrs. Bowden had caught up with him. They

stood at the top of a rocky cliff. All morning they had climbed. The mountain was steep and difficult. Several times they had saved themselves from falling only by pulling themselves up with handfuls of weeds or branches of trees. At midmorning Thomas had discovered a ridge wide enough for walking that seemed to circle to the east. Now he stood in dismay, nearly ready to cry. The ridge had narrowed and the way was blocked a little farther on by an impossibly large rock jutting out over a steep drop. Far below they could see a valley, inviting and green. A stream wound through it and disappeared from sight around the next hill. Thomas looked over the ledge. Even if they could make it over the cliff, the descent looked impossibly steep.

"Sit down and rest," Thomas told his mother. "I'll see if I can find an easier way down."

Mrs. Bowden looked back along the trail they had just made. "Thomas, wait," she said. Although they had not seen the wolves for hours, they knew they were still near. "I think we need to stay together," she said. "Are you sure we can't get past the rock?" She pointed. "Maybe we can climb a little above it and get past that way."

"Do you think we're strong enough to try?" he

asked. He knew that no matter how difficult it was for himself and Emma, it was even worse for his mother carrying Ben. He inched his way along the ridge. A few minutes later he halted. "Listen, do you hear that?"

"It sounds like water," Emma cried.

The ledge narrowed. They crept along, trying not to look down. "If this gets any worse, we will have to turn back," Thomas said. He glanced at his mother, but she waved him on. "I'm doing all right," she said.

Emma, inching along in the middle, almost seemed to be enjoying the climb. She was fearful of wolves and Indians and even tiny leeches. But looking over the sheer dropoff did not seem to worry her at all. She scrambled along as though she had been climbing mountains all her life.

Thomas was still holding Nobbin's leash, but he needed both hands to hang on to the rocky walls. And what if Nobbin somehow managed to entangle the line around his feet, as he often did? Balancing himself with one hand, he bent over and untied the leash from Nobbin's neck.

"Can Nobbin make it?" Emma asked.

"Oh, dogs are really surefooted," Thomas said, hoping it was true. As if to prove the point, Nobbin padded along steadily behind him. Step by step they inched along. Finally, they reached the huge boulder, and Thomas discovered his mother was right. Several smaller boulders provided a way to make the climb. As Thomas pulled himself up, he gave a gasp of delight. "There's a waterfall," he called down to his mother. Nobbin scrambled after him, and then Emma. Thomas climbed back to the top of the boulder to help his mother and Ben across.

A small stream fell in a series of cascades down the mountain. A cool spray of water splashed over them as they scrambled over the boulders.

"We could go that way," Emma said, pointing. The rocks along the waterfall were almost like a staircase leading down the mountain.

Thomas grinned. Emma was right. It was steep, but it looked like an easy climb down.

Nobbin waded in the little pool under the waterfall and lapped up the water. Thomas stretched over some rocks and brought a handful of water to his mouth. It was cold and sweet. He drank greedily. Nearby, Mrs. Bowden and Emma did the same.

"This would be a good place for a picnic," Emma said. She added wistfully, "Of course, we'd need some food."

"I was so scared back there on the ledge that I almost forgot about being hungry," Thomas admitted.

"It is beautiful here," Mrs. Bowden said. She slipped the baby from her shoulders and stretched her back. "Let's rest for a few minutes before we start down." She pointed across the valley. They were still in mountainous country, but the hills in the distance seemed smaller and less wild. "I think we may be past the worst of it," she said.

FOURTEEN

Bear!

Emma squinted at Thomas, shading her eyes from the bright sun with her hand. "Did you think we'd make it off that ledge?"

Thomas shrugged. "I guess I tried not to think about it, but I wasn't sure."

Their mother finished with the baby and stood beside them. She was pale, but she was smiling, and Thomas knew she was also feeling relieved.

Refreshed, they started again. By following the stream as it splashed its way down the mountainside, the travelers were able to reach the valley floor in a short time. Several times the footing was so steep that they simply sat and bumped their way down, grabbing at saplings to slow their descent. Other times, they climbed over boulders and rocks, but always they stayed close to the stream.

Once they were off the mountain, the stream grew into a river as it meandered across the valley. "Let's follow it for a while," Thomas suggested.

Mrs. Bowden nodded. "Good idea. This looks like good farming land; maybe somebody has settled nearby."

"I wonder what they'll think when they see us," Emma said. She brushed a tangled curl off her forehead.

Thomas laughed. They were filthy, and their clothes were in tatters. "They'll think we've been fighting those wolves."

Emma gave a grunt of satisfaction. "I'd like to see those wolves even try to follow us down that mountain."

Mrs. Bowden cast a worried look at the sky. "It's going to be dark soon, and there don't seem to be many protected spots here. We need to get closer to those hills by nightfall."

Emma's smile faded. Her energy and good spirits suddenly disappeared. "How much farther must we go?"

"Just a little more," her mother coaxed.

"I don't think I can make it without food," Emma said.

Thomas understood how she felt. It took every bit of his strength to continue putting one foot in front of another.

Still, there was no choice but to go on, and at least the walking was easier now so they could make good time. Nobbin sniffed the ground and was off in a flash, following a scent.

"I hope Nobbin finds something to eat," Emma said dully.

Thomas plodded on. Then, rounding a bend in the river, he stopped and shouted for joy. "Look."

A small wild plum tree grew beside the water. The plums were tiny and not quite ripe. Thomas pulled down a branch and picked handfuls. They stuffed their mouths, laughing as the sourness made their mouths pucker. "Careful," warned Mrs. Bowden. "You don't want to make yourselves sick."

"Look over here," Emma shouted gleefully. She had discovered a berry thicket. In the fertile valley soil the berries had grown larger and were more flavorful than the tiny ones they had found in the hills. Or at least that was how it seemed to Thomas as he crammed them in his mouth, letting the purple juice run down his chin. His mother found some greens for them to munch on, and Thomas thought that no meal had ever seemed so delicious.

Mrs. Bowden smiled with berry-stained lips. "We really need to keep walking," she reminded them. Emma filled her pocket with plums and, with a groan, Thomas set out again. Although his stomach gurgled uncomfortably, for now, at least, it was not so empty.

Further up the riverbank the tall grass began to shake, and they heard a snuffing sound. "Oh, that Nobbin," Emma said with a smile. "I wonder what he's chasing now." Still smiling, she headed toward the sound. "Here, Nobbin," she called.

Suddenly a small, furry shape bounded out of the tall grass. Emma yelped in surprise and started to run. Then she paused.

"Look, Mama," Emma said softly. "It's a little bear. Isn't he sweet?" She squatted down and held out her hand for the bear cub to smell.

"No!" Mrs. Bowden and Thomas shouted almost at the same instant.

Startled, Emma stood up and turned toward them. "It's just a baby," she protested.

Thomas remembered a trip he'd taken with his father to purchase supplies. A trader had poled a flatboat up the river, loaded with sugar, salt, cloth, and tools for the settlers to buy. On one side, the man looked like anybody else. But when he turned around, Thomas had seen that the hair on that side of his head was gone, a long scar ran down his face, and he wore a patch over that eye. The man had caught him staring. He leaned down close to Thomas and pointed to his head. "Mama bear," he said in a gravelly voice. "Touched her baby. This was her way of letting me know she didn't like it."

Remembering, Thomas looked around anxiously. The baby bear stopped and was giving them a quizzical look. "Back away, Emma," he said urgently.

"Why?" Emma asked. "He's too little to hurt anyone."

"You heard your brother," Mrs. Bowden snapped. "Back away from it now."

Hearing the urgency in her mother's voice, Emma obeyed, but she frowned.

"I don't know why everyone is so upset," she said as she reached them.

"Baby bears have mothers," Thomas hissed. "*Big* mothers."

Emma's mouth made a little O, and her eyes widened with understanding.

"Where do you suppose she is?" Mrs. Bowden whispered. "We don't want to run right into her."

Thomas was still, his mind working frantically. The nearest trees were some distance away. Thomas was pretty sure that bears could climb trees anyway. He looked at the bear cub. Perhaps, if they crossed the river, its mother wouldn't follow when she saw the cub was unhurt.

He explained his thinking to his mother. Mrs. Bowden nodded in agreement. Picking up her skirts, she waded in. The river was about thirty feet across and the water came up only to their knees. Thomas could see the marks on the banks where the water had been much deeper, probably in the spring when the winter snows had melted. This late in the summer the river was low. He and Emma quickly followed their mother. They climbed up the opposite bank and looked back at the bear cub. He was still sitting in the same spot. His head was cocked to one side and he looked puzzled as he watched them.

"He really is sweet," Emma said softly.

Thomas smiled in agreement. Then his smile faded. The cub had begun walking toward the river as though he would come after them. The Bowdens moved quickly away.

Thomas had almost breathed a sigh of relief when the little cub squealed. A second later they heard a fearful roar of anger, and a huge black bear came charging through the grass. She only hesitated a moment at the riverbank before plunging in, heading straight at them.

Thomas knew it was useless to run. He bent down and picked up several large stones from the stream. Mrs. Bowden and Emma, seeing what he had done, armed themselves with stones and stood beside Thomas. The bear was so close that Thomas could smell her strong, musty odor. She roared her challenge and Thomas could see teeth that were sharp and yellow, but it was her claws that frightened him the most. He could almost feel the scrape of them across his skin.

"Go away," screamed Mrs. Bowden.

The bear reared up on its hind legs, but it seemed to hesitate. "Make some noise," shouted Thomas. He banged the rocks together, screaming along with his mother. After a second, Emma banged her stones and yelled with them.

The baby bear splashed after his mother with a happy-sounding squeal. Then, as quickly as it had started, the attack was over. Roaring a final warning, the mother dropped back down on all fours and sniffed her cub, as if to reassure herself that it was unharmed. Then she cuffed the baby, sending it tumbling end over end. Unhurt, the little bear rolled back up and chased after its mother. They watched as the pair crossed the tall grass and disappeared into the forest.

But there was no time to enjoy their victory. As Thomas dropped his stones, he heard a voice behind him and froze.

"Well, if that don't beat everything," a man's voice said. "A woman and two younguns scaring off an old she-bear. I wouldn't have believed it if I hadn't seen it with my own eyes."

FIFTEEN

Safe at Last

Thomas turned slowly. The man was standing only a few feet away. It seemed as if he had appeared out of nowhere. His britches were dirty and torn, and over them he wore a deerskin tunic that reached nearly to his knees. His hair was tied back, Indian style, with a leather thong. He was not an Indian, in spite of his dress. Thomas saw blue eyes over his thick gray beard. He had a rifle casually draped over one arm.

The man saw Thomas looking at the rifle. He grinned, showing a mouthful of rotten and broken teeth. "I was 'bout ready to shoot that old bear. But you didn't need my help." He cackled wildly, slapping his free hand on his pants. Little clouds of dust filled the air. "Old Martha's not going to believe this," he said.

Mrs. Bowden had not spoken. Now she seemed to shake herself awake. "I'm Ellen Bowden and these are my children. We escaped a massacre across the mountains, and we've been walking for days without food. Is there a town nearby where I might get some help?"

"A massacre, you say?" The man looked straight at Thomas. "Just who was doing the killing?"

There was no way to tell if the man was a Tory or not. Maybe he hadn't even heard of the war for independence, living so far back in the hills. Thomas took a chance on the truth. "Indians," he said. "And Tories."

The man's eyes narrowed, and for a moment Thomas thought he had made a mistake. "Then you be patriots?"

Numbly, Thomas nodded.

"We are heading to Philadelphia to stay with my sister," Mrs. Bowden said. "My husband is nearby with General Washington's army."

The man nodded, as though satisfied with their answers. "Then you haven't heard the news," he said. "The British have withdrawn from Philadelphia. General Washington left a few men to guard the city. The rest of his army is following the redcoats. Was a big battle near Monmouth, New Jersey. Now General Washington is chasing them all the way back to New York."

Mrs. Bowden sagged weakly. Thomas grabbed her before she fell. After a minute she seemed better. "I-I'm sorry. It's just that I expected to see my husband soon."

The man's homely face looked gentle. "Don't you worry, Mrs. Bowden. General Washington is a good commander. I'm sure your husband is all right."

Mrs. Bowden stood up straighter and nodded.

"My cabin's not far. I'll take you there and old Martha will cook you up some food. Then, if you want, tomorrow I'll guide you to Stroud's settlement. It's not far from here. Someone there will take you on to Philadelphia."

"That's very kind of you, sir," Mrs. Bowden said.

"No need to be calling me sir," the man said. "My name's Sam. Sam Tucker."

"Wait, Mama," Emma said. "Where's Nobbin?

We can't go without Nobbin. You don't think that bear hurt him, do you?"

As if he'd been waiting to hear his name, Nobbin suddenly appeared on the opposite bank. With only a little coaxing, he splashed into the river and crossed to the other side. Then he shook himself, spraying tiny droplets of water over everyone.

Sam Tucker set off at a fast walk. With only a slight hesitation, Mrs. Bowden struck out after him. As they walked, Mr. Tucker asked questions about the massacre, listening carefully to Mrs. Bowden's account.

"When word of this gets out, people will be outraged. There are still a lot of people who haven't made up their minds about the war. Maybe this will persuade them to come to our side," Sam Tucker remarked.

Thomas and Emma trailed along behind. "He's a horrid-looking man, don't you think?" Emma whispered.

"I don't care," Thomas said. "If he gives us some real food, I'd follow him anywhere."

Emma rubbed at her stomach. "I don't feel very good. I wonder what Martha looks like," she added, rolling her eyes.

Mr. Tucker kept up a steady pace. At the end of an hour they came to a cabin, nearly hidden against the side of the hills. Several small children played outside. "Papa, Papa," they shouted gleefully as they ran to Sam Tucker. They hung back shyly when they saw their father was not alone. Sam Tucker scooped them up in a bear hug. At the same time a woman came to the door of the cabin. She was carrying a gun, but when she saw who it was, she leaned the gun up against the side of the house and came running.

Thomas watched Sam Tucker grab her and swing her around in a circle. In spite of his rough appearance, the man was obviously loved by his family.

"That's 'old' Martha?" Thomas whispered to Emma.

Martha was pretty, with dark brown hair and snapping dark eyes. Unlike her husband, she was clean and neatly dressed in a simple calico dress and apron. Sam Tucker spoke a few words to her, and she hurried over to greet them.

"I'm Martha Tucker," she said, putting her arm around Mrs. Bowden. "You just come right on in, and be welcome."

The cabin, Thomas noticed as they entered, was well kept and comfortable.

His mother looked puzzled, too, but she gratefully sat at a small table while Martha unfastened the apron sling from her back and laid Ben in a handmade cradle.

Martha admired the apron sling. "Isn't this clever," she said.

"Thomas thought of it," Mrs. Bowden said proudly.

Thomas blushed at the praise. "I just remembered seeing an Indian woman carrying a baby that way," he said.

"Sit down," Martha coaxed Emma and Thomas, and soon they were feasting on pieces of pork, some boiled potatoes, and warm slices of johnny-cake.

"After you eat, I'll heat up some water for a bath," Martha said.

The children, the oldest perhaps six or seven, crowded around, watching until their mother clapped her hands. "You quit bothering our company," she said as she shooed them back outside. "They don't see too many strangers," she apologized.

Sam Tucker seemed to have disappeared, but just as they finished eating he opened the door and came in. Thomas wasn't sure for a minute that it was the same man. This man was clean, and his beard was trimmed. When he smiled at their surprise, his teeth were white.

"The British soldiers don't pay much attention to old Sam Tucker," he said. "Makes it easy to hear things."

Thomas felt his mouth drop open. "You're a spy!" he said.

"Now I wouldn't say that," he said with a slow smile. "Spies can get themselves shot. But I do notice a few things as I travel around. Sometimes I talk with General Washington, and I tell him about the things I've seen. Matter of fact, I just might set out to visit him tomorrow. But first I'll take you to Stroud's settlement, like I promised. When I reach General Washington, I'll try to find your husband so I can tell him you're safely on your way to Philadelphia."

"Maybe we should go with you," Thomas suggested.

"I don't think that's a good idea," Sam Tucker

said. "There's not much fighting right now, but you never know."

"Do you think we will win?" Thomas asked.

Sam Tucker was silent for a long time. Then he nodded. "I do. And it's because of people like you."

"Like us?"

Sam Tucker nodded again. "One of these days the British are going to realize that we Americans are too tough to beat. They're going to give up and go home and let us have our freedom."

Thomas sat back, the watchfulness and fear draining away. Tomorrow they would continue their journey to Philadelphia. And after the war was over, maybe they would go back to their valley or even settle somewhere else. It would be a new country, and they were going to help it grow. He thought of all the people he'd met in the last few weeks—brave Eben and kind Mrs. Muldoon; the soldiers who had lost their lives; and Sam Tucker, who risked his. Most of all, he thought about his father, fighting for a dream. Freedom. Thomas smiled to himself. Now that was a word worth living for.

More about *Thomas*

The early American colonists were a restless people. Like the Bowdens, they pressed farther and farther west, always looking for new land and new opportunities. They crossed mountains, forded dangerous rivers, and tamed a wilderness. Nothing and no one stood in their way—not even the Native Americans who called the land their home.

These hardy settlers did not take well to being ruled by a king far across the ocean. When the call came, many men left their families to fight for freedom.

Not everyone agreed with the rebels' desire to rule themselves. Many colonists, though unhappy at the new taxes, remained loyal to the king. Those who joined the British army were called Tories.

It was a sad time in American history, with ugly incidents on both sides. Most of the Tories eventually fled the country. Some, like John Butler, who were chased from their homes by the patriots, formed armies to help the British. Some of the Indians, believing that the British would stop the colonists from taking more land, joined with them in attacks along the frontier. However, they soon learned that families just like the Bowdens were willing to sacrifice almost anything for freedom from British rule.

My story is based on a true incident—the massacre of colonists in Pennsylvania's Wyoming Valley. Thomas is a fictional character, and I have changed a few details to make the story more readable.

As I read the historical accounts of the Wyoming massacre, I was struck by the number of mistakes that led to the tragedy. If the soldiers had stayed in the fort, they might have been able to hold out until help arrived. If they had been more experienced, they might have recognized that they were being led into a trap. Many women and children died on the trek east after the fort's defeat, most lost in the swamps. Yet not one person who stayed in the fort was harmed. Although they were robbed of their possessions, John Butler allowed them to leave safely.

Here are some interesting facts about Thomas's time:

In the story, Thomas was bitten by gollynippers. Did you guess what they were? If you said *mosquitoes* you were right. Maybe they got their name when someone said, "Golly, something nipped me!"

There were no bees in America when the colonists first came. But some of the earliest settlers brought honeybees with them on ships. Swarms escaped into the forest, and by Thomas's time wild honey was a favorite treat. At first the settlers looked for "bee trees" and cut them down. Later, the farm women made crude hives, called *skeps,* out of coils of straw. Both were bad for the bees, though. The settlers took so much honey that the bees did not have enough food to live on through the winter. It was not until much later that hives were designed with sliding trays, so that enough honey was left for the bees.

A johnnycake was fried corn bread. Sometimes for a treat it was rolled in powdered sugar. At first they were called journey cakes, because people found them easy to carry for a snack as they traveled.

Boys and girls in Thomas's day were not very different from you. They liked to run and play tag, swim, play ball games, tell jokes, and argue with their brothers and sisters. But they also had to work. Most children started with simple chores when they were about five years old. By the time they were Thomas's age, they were expected to work nearly as hard as grown-ups. Boys chopped wood and helped to plow and plant and harvest. Girls worked just as hard in the home. In addition to cooking and cleaning, they churned butter, made soap, spun thread, cared for the vegetable garden, and watched younger brothers and sisters.